BRAVE ARE THE LONELY

BRAVE ARE THE LONELY

A Novel of World War II

JACK LANGLEY

iUniverse, Inc.
Bloomington

Brave Are the Lonely
A Novel of World War II

iUniverse books may be ordered through booksellers or by contacting:

iUniverse
1663 Liberty Drive
Bloomington, IN 47403
www.iuniverse.com
1-800-Authors (1-800-288-4677)

ISBN: 978-1-4759-9563-3 (sc)
ISBN: 978-1-4759-9565-7 (hc)
ISBN: 978-1-4759-9564-0 (ebk)

Library of Congress Control Number: 2013911582

Printed in the United States of America

iUniverse rev. date: 07/02/2013

Dedication

To my father, James F. Langley, Jr. 039940

Captain, United States Marines Corps

January 3, 1918-December 2, 1989

Member 4th Marine Division

Participant Battles of:

Roi-Namur

Saipan

Tinian

Iwo Jima

And to the gallant forces of U.S. Marines

Who fought and gave their lives in the cause of freedom.

Semper Fi

PROLOGUE

Jim Mathews grew up as an only child in a broken home. His mother had taken a job at the parish rectory to help make ends meet since his father, an uneducated man, made only a meager salary at the local cotton gin. It was many years later that Jim would come to understand why his parents had divorced when he was only seven years old, and why the parish priest suddenly left the ministry amidst a fiery scandal that involved the word "adultery". That event had driven his father to drink and an early death related to the use of illegal moonshine whiskey that he obtained from one of his fellow workers.

Jim and his mother had relocated to a small town near Little Rock, Arkansas where she performed odd jobs to provide for herself and her son. Jim also worked after school and on weekends to supplement their income. It left him little or no time for socializing even when he approached his final years in high school. It was the middle of the Great Depression and anyone with a job was happy to earn what little the job paid.

That summer, following graduation, on a whim Jim accepted an invitation to accompany a group of high school classmates in similar circumstances to a local Marine Corps recruiting station for a presentation on the benefits of joining the military . . . both immediate and long term.

There was talk of possible war in Europe but most Americans didn't feel that it would involve the United States if it came. There were also rumors of the Empire of Japan causing trouble somewhere in the Pacific. But at the beginning of the nineteen forties decade, the Orient was a long way off and a little understood part of the world.

Jim and the others liked what they heard and immediately decided that the Corps was their ticket out of the desperate circumstances of their lives. They inked their names to four year contracts and prepared to leave for Parris Island, South Carolina to begin boot camp on the last day of August of the year nineteen forty.

With the thoughts of possible war on the horizon, Jim's mother was fearful for him, but understood that joining the military was the manly thing for him to do. Hopefully it would prepare him for life and teach him a trade that could be put to good use after his time in service was complete. It would immediately remove him from the environment that she had come to hate, and from the clutches of the depression that showed no signs of abating. She was sure that she didn't want to see him follow in his father's miserable footsteps.

The events that would follow that fateful decision could not have been imagined, even if Jim or his family had been avid students of the military and the long and glorious history of heroes that often emerged during combat.

*Original 1944 planning map for the invasion of
Iwo Jima from the author's private collection.*

Iwo Jima Memorial, Arlington, Virginia. Photo by the author.

*"Among the men who fought on Iwo Jima,
uncommon valor was a common virtue."*

*Fleet Admiral Chester W. Nimitz
March 16, 1945*

CHAPTER ONE

It was late nineteen eighty-nine and the Christmas holidays were imminent. The trees were bare and a light frost still glimmered on the grass of the sprawling cemetery. A gentle wind that blew from the north only served to augment the already bone chilling cold of that somber December morning.

"I can't believe he's really gone!"

"C'mon, Mom. It's time to go. I don't want you to catch pneumonia standing out here too long."

Most of the congregation had long departed the gravesite that held the earthly remains of Jim Mathews. In the distance, the lone bugler who had provided a stirring rendition of "Taps", still stood at attention in United States Marine Corps full dress uniform, silhouetted against a solitary oak tree.

"He was such a quiet man. Most people never even knew what a brave and lonely soul he was.

Your father had many friends while in the military, but after he returned home from the war he abandoned most of them out of fear of losing them too I suspect. I don't think he ever got over what he saw there . . . or what he was called upon to do during his years in the Pacific. After he won the medal, he was asked to speak many times at soldier gatherings. Out of respect for his comrades, he did a few times right after returning home. But for the last forty or more years, he preferred not to talk about it."

"Did he ever confide in you about the war, Mom? I don't remember him ever mentioning it in my presence."

"Once.

He told me some things that were hard for him to say. You could see the tears well up in his eyes and hear the crackling of his voice whenever he tried to speak of those times over there, and the people he was with . . . especially the ones that never made it home.

I tried to tell him that I understood how difficult it must be to speak of such things. But, he assured me that no one could really know just how difficult it was unless they had been there.

I assured him that I was willing to listen to his stories at any time. I thought that after the years had allowed the strong emotions to fade a bit it would be easier for him. But, it never was.

When we visited cemeteries on Memorial Day, which we did faithfully every year, I often sensed that he wanted to tell me more . . . but he never did. We talked of taking a trip to the sites of the big Pacific battles with some of his Marine friends . . . but that too he put off for various reasons. I don't think he could have handled seeing the graves of his comrades or the places where they died even after so many years.

So now, those memories will all be buried with him."

Maria stood silently behind her mother for several minutes.

Finally, her mother released her hand from the coffin, took Maria's arm and prepared to go.

"Goodbye, my darling.

I'll miss you and I look forward to joining you soon."

She touched the coffin one last time and then threw a kiss toward Jim's grave as they turned to leave.

Maria was concerned about her mother's reference to her own mortality, but remained silent as they walked to the waiting limousine that would return them to the family home. As they passed the bugler, Helen gave a faint wave of thanks and forced a smile his way. He acknowledged her gesture with a crisp salute.

The women held hands tightly but didn't speak during the twenty minute ride back to the house. Safely inside the living room, Maria's mother burst into tears.

She stood and held her mother quietly, comforting her as best she could given the circumstances. Silently, she tried to imagine how her mother could go on without the man that she had loved and lived with for more than forty years. Helen sat down on her favorite chair. After a moment in which she attempted to compose herself, she turned to Maria.

"If you will look in our bedroom closet, your father kept a small safe in the corner on the floor. In it, you will find his medal in a small box.

Please bring it to me. I'd just like to look at it again. It's been a long time.

The safe should be unlocked."

Maria got up and walked to the bedroom.

In the back corner of the oversized walk-in closet, she saw the safe and swung open the door that was already ajar. She was surprised to find not only the small box with the Marine Corps insignia atop a silhouette of the medal contained within, but also a large brown envelope addressed to her mother.

Returning to the living room, she handed the objects to her mother.

"I found this addressed to you along with the box containing the medal."

Helen carefully inspected the envelope that bore her name written in her husband's easily recognizable handwriting.

"I never saw this before. He must have placed it there just recently without telling me. Would you open it for me?"

Maria took the envelope and carefully unsealed it.

It contained several sets of VCRs each in their own case. Accompanying the tapes was a handwritten letter. A quick glance at the last page revealed her father's signature.

"The letter's from Dad and it's addressed to you."

"Please read it to me. I don't think I can. My eyes are still wet."

Maria unfolded the pages, glanced once more toward her mother and began reading.

"My darling Helen,

Since you're reading this, it means that I am gone. I know that I wasn't always the best husband through the years, and that you must think me selfish for not sharing more things with you. But you must understand just how difficult it was for me to be candid about some of the things that happened to me during my time in the Pacific war.

3

Now, I would like to set the record straight.

I've spent a good deal of time putting together the VCRs that accompany this letter. I know it won't make up for my silence over the years, but I hope that it will at least explain why I did what I felt I had to do . . . my way. Maria is probably standing next to you as you read this . . . or perhaps she is reading it to you. Either way, know that I loved you both dearly and please forgive me for my ways.

Now, if you will play the VCR that has your name on it, I hope you will better understand the part of me that has remained silent through the years.

All my love forever,

Jim

P.S. The case marked with your name is for you only. It's a little personal. The other set of tapes is ok to show to whomever you choose."

Maria looked at her mother.

"You didn't know anything about this?"

"No.

Your father often went out by himself . . . for walks or occasionally to play golf or so he said.

I guess he was working on it during those times. But, he must have had someone help him make the VCRs . . . I doubt he could do it all by himself. He was never very handy with electronic things."

She smiled . . . in fact, almost laughed for a brief moment.

Maria remained quiet for several moments while her mother reminisced.

"Why he had trouble just changing channels on the T.V. when we got our first remote. He would make excuses about people getting lazy and get up to change a channel like we used to do. And when we got our first VCR . . . I thought he was going to break the darn thing . . . he got so frustrated trying to get it to work."

Helen took out a tissue and wiped her eyes, still wet from the emotional events of the day.

Finally, Maria asked: "Are you ready to watch this, Mom?"

"I think so."

Maria led her mother into the den where they had a large screen T.V. with an attached VCR player. She loaded the first cassette into the machine and sat down next to her Mom.

"Well, here goes" she said as she pressed the play button.

The opening frame had a written dedication with a voiceover narrated by her husband:

"This is the story of my life in the United States Marine Corps. I was proud to be the recipient of numerous awards, most especially the Congressional Medal of Honor.

However, I want everyone who sees and hears my story to understand that the medal, while it bears my name, belongs to each and every person in my squad who was there with me during those days on Iwo Jima so many years ago. Many of them received lesser awards. Many of them received no personal recognition at all.

All of them died in combat.

By being awarded the medal, I was relieved of further combat duties and was protected during the remaining months of a conflict that ended with victory after many hard won battles and far too many casualties.

So to my comrades in arms from that conflict so many years ago . . . especially to the members of my squad, to the 4th Marine Division and others who took part in the battle of Iwo Jima . . . and to their families, I say with great pride one last time:

'Semper Fi'"

As the frames advanced, she was surprised to see her husband standing in full military uniform, complete with medals.

Around his neck hung the unmistakable blue ribbon with a field of white stars that supported the highest ranking tribute of our nation given to someone in uniform known as the Congressional Medal of Honor.

He stepped to the center of the frame where he had a microphone positioned and began.

"Helen . . . and Maria if you are there too . . . I know that you will find it hard to believe that someone who has always been shy like me had the presence of mind to put something like this together. When I found out that I had cancer and possibly only a short time left to live, I decided to create this for you and for future generations of our family. As I indicated in the dedication, it's not just to remember me and the honors I received for my service in World War II . . . but for all my comrades in arms who lived and died in service to this great country of ours.

Many times during the last year when I left the house to 'visit a friend' or 'play golf', I was actually working on this project. Of course I had a great deal of help from my friends at the local library, as well as from the military historians I communicated with in Washington and from an old golfing buddy who just happened to know a lot about making professional VCR recordings.

To all of them I am eternally grateful.

Many the time I wanted to confide in you about my project, but somehow I think it best that it worked out this way.

So, here is my story!"

Chapter Two

*The nineteen thirty-nine/nineteen forty school year was a terrible one for me.
It was my last year in high school and my grades were doing poorly thanks
mostly to my need to work. Even though we had moved closer to Little Rock,
word of the scandal followed us.*

*Ever since Mom's affair with the priest and her breakup from Dad, and
then his death, things had gone from bad to worse. It was almost like she
was that woman Hester Prynne in "The Scarlet Letter". She was ridiculed
and laughed at. We could hardly go anywhere without someone pointing
their finger at her. And the kids in school wouldn't have much to do with
me either. I sometimes heard them whisper the word 'whore'. At first I didn't
know what it meant; when I got older and understood what they were
saying, it made me real mad. I got in fights with others all the time and
that kept me in trouble at school with the teachers and the school principal,
even though I'm sure they realize now that they could have been a little more
understanding.*

*Mom did whatever she could to make ends meet, but it was always hard.
The only work she could get were jobs that others mostly wouldn't do, like
cleaning bathrooms in gas stations or stores. The pay was bad back then . . .
usually not more than a dollar a day . . . and frequently much less. We didn't*

have any minimum wage laws like today. Of course the house was small, and the rent and utilities weren't much. But still, after buying food and clothes, there was hardly anything left over for us to spend just for fun.

I found that there were lots of odd jobs for high school students . . . if you didn't mind the odd hours and sometimes getting your hands dirty. So I decided that it was my responsibility to help out and hopefully let Mom enjoy life a bit. She was getting older and her legs were about to give out from all the mopping and scrubbing she did, mostly on her hands and knees.

A friend of our minister who knew of our desperate situation asked me if I could do some work for him at his trucking company. It involved loading and unloading freight trucks. It was pretty hard work and it didn't pay much, but the worst part was I had to work from three a.m. until about seven-thirty a.m. Then I went right to school from there. I was tired most of the time, so my grades started to slip.

Another member of our church who owned a variety store in town also was aware of our situation and asked if I could help out for a few weeks before Christmas when one of his regular salespeople got sick. I did a good job for him so he let me work as many Saturdays as I could up until I left town. That was about the time when Mom was not feeling well, so it kept us going until she got back on her feet. Then after graduation I was about to take a job at the mill where my father had worked. And that's when fate stepped in.

Some boys I barely knew from high school were heading to the Marine Corps recruiting station in Little Rock for a meeting with the sergeant there. They asked me to come along even though we didn't know each other very well. The things we had in common were our bad grades and our bad tempers. But at least we had graduated.

The sergeant was real friendly and said he was sure there was a place for each of us in the Corps. It meant that we were guaranteed to be paid every month and I could send part of it home to my mother. Well, I bought his sales pitch lock, stock and barrel . . . signed the papers right then and there. I had already turned eighteen, so I didn't need my mother's permission. Two others signed later.

Funny thing is, out of the six of us that went there that day, only two of us became Marines. One of the others joined the Navy, and two later went into the Army and died in Europe. I was the only one that survived the war in the Pacific. The guy that joined the Navy became a medic and was on board the Bismarck Sea when she was sunk off Iwo Jima during the air assault by the Japanese a day or two after the initial landing.

I felt real bad about losing all of them for a long time since it was their idea and not mine to join the military in the first place. But I realized long ago that life must go on . . . and I was lucky enough to meet you later on and that made all the difference in my life.

But on with the story.

The three of us who opted for the Marines were assigned to Parris Island, South Carolina for boot camp. I sure wish that someone would have warned me about just how tough it would be. I was like the other guys who looked at pictures of recruiting posters and saw a Marine in dress blues and thought how neat he looked, but didn't really consider all that he had been through to get to that point in his career.

Fortunately, I was pretty athletic so I spent the few weeks I had before reporting doing some running and working out. The guy that didn't get through basic . . . well, he was a little on the hefty side and never had been into sports or running. They put him on a diet and made him do extra running and exercising. He was doing great until he went and broke his ankle during a rappelling exercise during the fourth week. The doctors felt that he would never be able to resume basic and he was given a medical discharge.

I hope he knows just how lucky he was. Last I heard, he had a business of his own and a family and grandchildren. But, he probably knows that and counts his lucky stars every day and every night.

At least I hope he does.

ᗤ

Well, the big day came, and Bob and I . . . you remember Bob Plunckett? . . . he dated your friend Betty when we first met in Washington . . . well we got on that bus at the recruiting station and rode together to Parris Island.

We were barely off the bus, when our drill instructor met the group and introduced himself as Sergeant Monty Anderson. I happened to be first in line when he approached us.

"What's your name son?"

He shouted so loud it scared the hell out of me.

"Jim Mathews", I answered timidly.

"Whenever you speak to me, you will address me as Drill Sergeant Anderson. When asked, you will state your last name first, followed by your first name.

Do you hear me?" He looked about as mean as a bulldog about to bite someone.

He rotated his head from side to side as he spoke indicating he was addressing the whole group.

"Yes sir."

We all learned to answer in unison real fast.

"Yes sir, who?"

"Yes sir, Drill Sergeant Anderson."

"I can't hear you", he roared back at us.

We learned to shout the answers to him . . . he must have been a little hard of hearing after all the shouting that went on all the time.

"Yes sir, Drill Sergeant Anderson" we all bellowed.

"Much better."

He then turned back to me.

"Now, son. What is your name?"

Well, I shouted just as loud as I could:

"Mathews, Jim, Drill Sergeant Anderson."

"I think you just might just be a fast learner, Mathews.

The rest of you can learn from him!

Now, grab your things and fall in."

Now mind you, things in those days were a whole lot different than today. The military was already gearing up for war . . . we just didn't quite understand that at first. Boot camp had been reduced to only six weeks in length earlier that year because of the possibility of war and the need to build up their reserves. We followed the sergeant to our barracks where things got moving real fast. With only six weeks to train us, there wasn't time for all the niceties that recruits get today during the first week.

"I'm going to show you to your racks (that's Marine Corps lingo for a bunk), get you some real GI clothes and treat each of you to a haircut. Then we'll get you some chow and later on we'll have a GI party."

Well, right off the bat we all thought he was trying to be a nice guy since we showed him we were fast learners.

We should have known better.

We barely had time to put our things in the foot locker provided at the foot of each rack, when we were hustled off to the barber shop. By the time we got through, we were all bald and you could hardly tell one of us from the other. It sure would have been easy to learn how to cut hair there . . . you only needed to know one style.

After we learned how to chow down in less than ten minutes, we were off to get our new clothes . . . dungarees and t-shirts. They also issued us our backpacks, canteens, web belts, poncho, field jacket and gloves. As soon as we were in uniform for the first time, Drill Sergeant Anderson gave us our first talk about military rules. Article eighty-six of the Uniform Code of Military Justice prohibits absence without leave. Article ninety-one prohibits disobedience to a lawful order. And article ninety-three prohibits disrespect to a senior officer. He made sure we understood that those rules were absolute and non-breakable and that there were serious consequences if you did.

We all got that message real fast.

Court-martial was the penalty for breaking those rules.

Then we ran all the way back to the barracks where a GI party awaited us . . . just another way of saying we were going to clean the barracks . . . our home for the next six weeks . . . until it was so clean you could eat off the floor. Each time we had a "party", one poor guy was lucky enough to have to scrub the toilet with a toothbrush. I wasn't so lucky the first time, but my turn came up often enough.

Early the next morning . . . actually it was still the middle of the night as far as I was concerned . . . at about three a.m., the sergeant and his fellow drill instructors came tearing into the barracks, flashing the lights and yelling.

"All right you sleepyheads . . . time to rise and shine.

Or were you planning on sleeping all day?"

Well, we jumped up out of our racks and yelled "No sir, Drill Sergeant Anderson" at the top of our lungs.

"Very good!

You're learning faster than the last group to come through here. It took them almost a week to learn how to answer properly. Just for that, we're only going to do a one mile hike today . . . after our warm up calisthenics. When we return, we'll have a good hot breakfast and then you're going to be issued your rifles and learn some hand-to-hand combat. If you're lucky, we'll finish by ten . . . p.m. that is."

I looked at Bob and it seemed he was about to get sick just thinking about all that exercising and marching.

"Now, form up into three squads and let's get moving."

Sergeant Anderson had his two junior drill instructors help us form into three groups by alphabetical order. That put Bob and me in different groups.

As soon as our squads were all in line, he had us walk in formation . . . then run as soon as we got the hang of it. He marched along side of us shouting "Hup Hup, Hup," in order to keep us in step. And just as soon as we got back from our mile run, we went straight to the mess hall and had that breakfast he promised. Now I was never a big breakfast eater at home, but after that workout, I ate everything they put on the plate.

Then they took us to a big room where we were given our M1 rifles. It was a .30 caliber semi-automatic weapon designed in 1932 by John Garand and was often referred to by his last name only. It stayed in use until the late 1950's and is still used in some drilling classes.

First they gave us a demonstration of how to "field strip" . . . that means clean . . . your weapon. Next Sergeant Anderson himself told us of the Marine Corps rifle creed. He was real solemn when he said that we must treat that rifle like it was our best friend. Why that rifle was no good without the man that owned it and learned how to use it for the purpose that it was made . . . to kill the enemy before the enemy killed him.

During our time in training and beyond we were to keep that weapon clean and ready to use at all times because it was to become an integral part of each of us. They had us practice taking it apart and putting it back together again so many times that we all thought we could do it blindfolded. But in fact we found out we weren't quite ready when they made us try to do it just that way . . . blindfolded.

Sergeant Anderson assured us that before our training was over we would all be able to do just that . . . or we wouldn't graduate. So we kept practicing until we were able to do it with our eyes closed.

"When are we going to get to shoot our weapons Drill Sergeant Anderson?" one recruit made the mistake to ask.

Well, he turned toward that soldier and in the most serious tone we had heard to that point said in an extra loud voice for us all to hear:

"You'll learn soon enough to shoot your weapon. First you need to know everything about it and how to keep it operational at all times.

And learn this now: when you need to use it in combat, the enemy will be pointing his weapon at you, trying to kill you just as you will be trying to kill him."

I guess he made his point because no one ever asked that question again. The prospect of actual combat was becoming more real each day.

Well, that was our first full day as recruits and we were sure glad when it was over. After that, we counted out the days until completion of basic training knowing that each day brought us closer to becoming real Marines and to live action.

Chapter Three

For someone who had been friendless and lonely most of my life, from the days when mother went to work to supplement my father's meager pay, to the days after my parents divorce and mother worked out of sheer necessity, things were quite different for those six weeks. I actually got to the point that I would have welcomed a little peace and quiet.

The bathroom in the barracks had no privacy at all. I wasn't used to using a toilet or taking a shower where everyone could see your every move. I still remember our first day there when we were taught how to bathe by Drill Sergeant Anderson. He stood right in the shower stall with us . . . made us all strip off all our clothes . . . then showed us the military way to bathe. You first get all wet; then you take a bar of soap and lather it up and wash your face, then rinse your face; then you lather one arm and rinse that arm and . . . well you get the picture. You'd think we had never taken a shower before. In truth, there were a few guys in our squad that I honestly don't think knew what taking a shower meant before joining the corps.

Well, we bathed together, ate together, trained together, slept together and learned how to take care of our rifles together; in short, it was like one big family that never learned how to do anything alone. But by the time we finished our six weeks training, we understood that was exactly the point of it all: to learn to function as one cohesive unit and to obey our superiors without question.

By the second week we were marching in unison like real Marines. During the third week we finally got to fire our weapons on the rifle range and learn some basic assault tactics. We were broken up into five-man squads to see how we functioned in smaller groups and I was designated our squad "corporal" . . . meaning that I gave the orders during our training exercises.

Well, I guess our squad did all right because when we got our evaluations, we had won top prize. The drill instructor gave us an evening off for that . . . the first time since we arrived in Parris Island that we actually had time to breathe and do something of our own choosing. It was the first time I had a chance to sit down and write my mother and let her know that I was doing well and that I thought of myself as "almost a Marine".

The rest of the time just flew by, although the final big test they call "the Crucible" . . . I guess it's named after the container that metals are heated in to their melting point . . . made all of us nervous while we waited for it to begin . . . but we passed and when it was done we were sure we were going to be Marines. It's a three day and night exercise that tests everything we had learned since day one. It had some funny named parts like "Jenkins Pinnacle" and "Garcia's Engagement". But the whole thing was designed to make us work together as a unit to solve problems based on facts we had been taught earlier in the course. It involved lots of walking and running and carrying heavy backpacks . . . but included time for chow and rest.

In Jenkins Pinnacle there are two horizontal logs at just enough distance apart so that you can't jump from one to the other . . . and there is water and mud in the space between. So the team has to design a way across in a short period of time. Well, we showed them. We found a sturdy enough branch from a pine tree and straddled the two. The smallest member of the team walked across it and then was able to help each of us jump most of the distance with a pull from him standing near the opposite end of the branch. Not one of us even got our feet wet. Then we disposed of the branch so that the group behind us would have to figure it out for themselves.

Garcia's engagement involves hand-to-hand combat training followed by a warrior case study of the real Private Garcia. We passed that one with flying colors too.

Years later when I thought back to those days I realized that it was the most valuable training I ever had in my life . . . and undoubtedly responsible for saving my life in combat. In retrospect, it was actually easier than real combat where you generally don't have time for the basics of life and you know people are trying to kill you for real.

But finally Drill Sergeant Anderson rounded us up the day after "the Crucible" . . . after we had gotten some rest . . . and told us we all had passed and would graduate the following week.

Well! I almost felt like hugging him.

But being the squad "corporal", I ordered my men to stand at attention; we saluted him and thanked him for getting us through. I almost thought I saw him smile for the first time since we got off that bus only a few weeks earlier and I was introduced to him in a baptism of fire.

The day of our graduation was bright and sunny and we were all so proud when we marched in front of the commandant and all the visiting dignitaries that had come from Washington and other commands. But mostly I was proud that mother was able to come all the way from Arkansas. She hadn't ever been out of the state in her entire life. It would have been nice if my father had been alive to see me in my uniform . . . but considering all that happened between him and Mom, I guess it was just as well.

I had been able to use some of my pay to buy Mom a round trip bus ticket to Beaufort, South Carolina . . . the small town nearest to Parris Island . . . and to arrange a place for her to stay. The trip kind of wore her out since it took almost three days from Little Rock. In those days, the buses stopped in just about every big or little town along the way. She really looked bedraggled when she arrived.

But on the morning of our graduation, she looked real nice in her Sunday finest dress and hat. She was so proud that I had made it through basic training, but I could tell that like most mothers, she was now more worried than ever that I was closer to real danger since things around the world had been heating up even more just since I began basic training.

We got ten days leave after graduation, so I took the bus home to Arkansas with mother. She was kind of forlorn looking, knowing she might not see me again for a long while . . . or never if war broke out and something were to happen to me. I couldn't help but notice that she was looking older. Her hair had turned gray and her face had wrinkled a lot. She tried to hide it the best she could, but her energy was going too and she needed help just walking any distance. The divorce and the treatment she received after people learned of her affair with the priest had been trying enough. And Dad's death.

And now this.

I thought when I left to join the corps that it would ease her problems somewhat since I could provide some help supporting her. But now I realized that I was just adding to her worries. If we had just had some close relatives to help her at home I would have felt better about having to leave her.

When we arrived back home, I was relieved to find that there were some neighbors that had befriended her and expressed concern for her welfare. They offered to help out with any needs she might have in my absence. I was pleased too that they were proud that I had joined the military in these trying times. Even though President Roosevelt tried to assure the nation that we weren't going to war during one of his fireside chats, most everyone knew that it was inevitable. At the time though we assumed it would be with Germany and her allies. No one seriously thought much about Japan attacking us considering the distance between the Japanese mainland and the U.S. or its territories.

I had been assigned to the infantry training course at Quantico, Virginia after my leave was up, so it didn't give me much time at home. It took me another three days to get back just in time to report, so I had to say goodbye to my mother, never knowing if we would see each other again if war should break out.

She cried as I mounted the bus steps . . . in fact, she had been crying since the day before. She tried to say everything a mother wants to say to her son going off in the military and possibly to war. It was heart wrenching for both of us.

But I promised I would write her just as often as I could . . . and I kept that promise to the day she died . . . unfortunately during the Saipan campaign . . . so I never saw her alive again and didn't even get to attend her funeral.

Well, here I was at Quantico, Virginia. For a boy from rural Arkansas, I was already realizing that I would get to see the world a little piece at a time. Of course, at that point in time, I had no idea just how much of the world that would eventually include.

The course was tough, but after basic at Parris Island, I and my fellow Marines felt we could handle anything . . . and we did. We practiced all the things that we had been taught in basics, plus various assault maneuvers, especially beach landings. We were beginning to understand by this time that being combat troops wasn't the fun that we somehow imagined watching war movies. This was serious business and people actually got killed. We practiced with live ammunition being aimed over our heads. It was pretty scary stuff at the beginning. After a short while we kind of got used to it, but our company sergeant, a WWI veteran assured us that we better take it all very seriously if we wanted to survive the real thing.

It was there that Bob Plunkett and I were together again for another short six weeks. After that we wouldn't meet again. He was assigned to the 1st Marine Division and I eventually became a part of the newly organized 4th. He made it all the way through the war and then got killed in the waning months during the invasion of Okinawa in April, 1945.

"Bob, what do you say we go into D.C. for the weekend? It's only about thirty-five miles and I hear they have bus service right to the center of town. Some of the fellows in my barracks know some girls they can fix us up with."

"Sounds good to me, Jim.

When do we leave?"

"The sergeant says we can go about six on Friday. I've checked and there's a bus at seven. There's a YMCA that we can stay at right near the bus terminal . . . that is, if we don't get lucky and get invited home by someone we meet."

Bob smiled. He was always a little shy anyway, kind of like me. I guess that's why we got along fairly well. So that Friday evening we were off to Washington for some fun, not knowing that fate had something special in store for me.

CHAPTER FOUR

The bus left Quantico about a half hour late, so it was going on eleven p.m. before we arrived in downtown Washington after making stops at Alexandria and Arlington en route. It was my first time there and it was thrilling to see everything so lit up even at that late hour. I was especially awed by the sight of the U.S. capitol building with its glowing dome and the Washington monument illuminated by a circle of floodlights at its base.

When we stepped off the bus we were met by about a dozen girls. Most of them seemed to be looking for a good time, if you know what I mean? But Bob and I were hoping to meet some nice girls who could show us a good time in the city and not be just one night stands.

Wally, that was one of the guys from the barracks that asked us if we wanted to go to D.C., introduced us to two of the girls who appeared to be a little more shy than the others. And that was just fine with Bob and me.

Their names were Helen and Betty. Betty was about five feet four with auburn hair, a natural smile and a pleasant figure. Helen was the most beautiful thing that I had ever seen . . . about five six with light auburn hair, hazel eyes and the most radiant smile and perfect teeth like you would expect to see in a toothpaste commercial.

I was smitten right away.

I walked right up to her and introduced myself.

"I'm Jim Mathews and this is my friend Bob Plunkett. We're attending the infantry training program at Quantico, Virginia.

We're Marines!"

I forgot to mention that we were in civvies. Our C.O. had given us permission to go into town without having to wear our uniforms.

Helen's response was that she figured something like that since the bus said "U.S. Marine Corps" on the side. Well, I liked her sense of humor right from the start. And it made me think that she was probably pretty smart as well.

"I'm Helen Brand and this is my friend, Betty Champagne . . . and before you make any jokes about that, consider that her mother's maiden name was Drinkwine!"

Bob and I stood silent for a moment. We didn't know whether to laugh or not . . . but when we couldn't hold it any longer, we both did . . . and they both joined in the merriment.

"You're not serious?

That was really your mother's maiden name?" I said looking at Betty.

"Dead serious.

Believe me, it's been the subject of lots of jokes.

People always want to label me as having a 'bubbly personality' or being a 'real corker'. One guy said if I were champagne, he'd like to be on my case. And there were a few more that were downright risqué. Well, you get the point. I'll be curious to see what you fellows come up with."

Bob and I just stood staring. We just felt lucky to be standing here with these two lovely girls and I didn't want to say anything stupid that might turn them off. But Bob couldn't help himself and led off with "why don't you pour me a glass or two and let's see if you're really that bubbly when uncorked."

Betty glared at him, but then seemed to melt when he gave her one of his famous smiles. Helen and I just stood there and held our breath. After a few minutes of silence, I was forced to speak.

"How about we get something to eat?" I offered.

Helen turned to Betty and smiled; the frown left her face and she nodded.

"That would be great. There's a nice little Italian restaurant just about a block down the street near Dupont Circle."

I guess I had a strange look on my face when Helen mentioned that name.

"Don't worry. You'll get used to Washington. It's full of circles, all with fancy names. And the big diagonal streets are mostly named for the states. The streets that run north and south are numbered and the ones that run east and west are named after the alphabet. There is no 'J' street for fear of confusion with 'I' . . . and 'I' street is usually spelled 'Eye' and 'Q' street 'cue' and well . . . you'll understand after a while I'm sure. So it's pretty easy to get around this big town and fairly hard to get lost once you get the hang of it."

She smiled as if she were sure we understood. Well, Bob and I weren't exactly sure whether her explanation had made it easier or harder to understand the street design.

So we just smiled back and nodded our heads.

Helen took me by the hand and Betty grabbed Bob and together they led us to Pasquales where we had the best Italian food I had ever tasted. Come to think of it, it was probably the first and only Italian food I had ever had . . . the last I recall there weren't many Italians in Arkansas.

Helen and Betty weren't what you would call "fast girls" and that was just fine. As I said, Bob and I were kind of shy and not used to being around women much. So after dinner and a lingering cup of coffee, they showed us to the YMCA down the street and headed home. Before leaving, Helen slipped me her phone number. Few people could afford a private phone in those days, but she said there was one in the boarding house parlor. So armed with that information, I told her I would call her the following morning. I'm not sure if she believed me or not, but I thought there was something between us from the first moment we met.

Well, the following morning it was raining and Bob and I slept in until noon. It had been a long time since we had the leisure of doing anything like that. By the time I had showered and dressed, it was almost one o'clock. The rain had stopped but it was still gloomy. I asked Bob if he would like to call the girls and see if they were interested in showing us around town. He wasn't exactly infatuated with Betty . . . he thought she talked too much and had a funny accent . . . she was from Connecticut after all and had a typical New England Yankee twang.

"Why don't we just do a little sightseeing on our own? I'd like to climb the Washington monument and see what the town looks like from the top."

I told him I would go with him but later I'd like to see if Helen would go out with me. He wasn't sure about asking Betty to go, but I convinced him that it would probably be better if we went as couples . . . I wasn't sure if Helen would say yes if Betty wasn't invited too.

So we went to the Washington monument. The bus left from right in front of the YMCA and took us to within a block of it. By the time we got there, the skies had finally begun to clear. I guess because of the weather, there weren't many people in line.

Well, I have to say walking up five hundred and fifty-five steps was a job even for a couple of in-shape Marines like us. Some folks we passed on the way up looked like they couldn't make it the rest of the way and probably should have considered walking back down. The different gifts from the states and various organizations that lined the steps were amazing to see. Being Marines, we were especially proud of our heritage and of the tributes to the founder of our country.

The view from the top observation platform was spectacular. We could see the capitol building, the White House, the Jefferson and Lincoln memorials and the Tidal Basin. The sun had come out and made everything shimmer after the rain soaking earlier in the day.

We took the elevator down. They had a small gift shop where there was a pay telephone. After some coaxing, Bob agreed to let me call the girls and see if they would join us for dinner and a movie.

Since it was almost four o'clock in the afternoon when I finally called, Helen confided that she was beginning to think that she might not hear from me again. I could tell by the tone of her voice that she was pleased to get my call, and I must confess that I was equally enthusiastic about hearing her voice on the other end. There was something about her expression that made me feel tingly inside. Betty agreed to come along, but I could tell from Helen's tone that she was not especially excited to see Bob again either.

"There's a small family restaurant just around the corner from our apartment building that I think you would like. It's fairly quiet so we can just sit and talk . . . and the food is good and inexpensive."

I suggested that we might enjoy a movie after dinner and that seemed to please her too.

"Have you seen 'The Grapes of Wrath'? Henry Fonda, that wonderful new young actor, stars in it."

Well, I didn't want to act totally ignorant, so I just said "no, I hadn't seen it yet". Confidentially, I had no idea who Henry Fonda was or what in God's name the movie was about. I guess I was expecting it to have something to do with making wine since it had the word "grape" in the title. At that point in time I had never really read any books other than what was required in school and if she had mentioned the name "John Steinbeck" I would really have shown my ignorance.

৵৴

The D.C. Diner (such an original name) was just as she had said . . . inexpensive with good food. However, it was anything but quiet. It was Saturday night after all and it seemed that everyone in town was out. Traffic outside the diner was brisk, both on the street and on the sidewalk, and inside you could hardly hear yourself think let alone understand someone else's conversation.

I reached under the table and held Helen's hand (we were sitting beside one another) and whispered into her ear "I think you're beautiful". For a moment I didn't think she had heard what I said with all the noise surrounding us.

Then she squeezed my hand and leaned into my ear and whispered back that she thought I was the most handsome man she had ever met. Well, I didn't know quite what to say to that. No one had ever called me handsome before . . . except mother. She leaned back and whispered again. This time she suggested that she and I go for a walk by ourselves and meet up with Bob and Betty later. I wasn't sure how Bob would take that . . . I mean leaving him alone with Betty . . . but I didn't much care at that point. I had found myself a girl that really seemed to like me and I knew I liked her . . . and well, we needed to see just where things would take us. So we excused ourselves and walked out onto Connecticut Avenue.

The rain and clouds earlier in the day had moderated the temperatures so we found ourselves walking along on a cool clear October evening with a big harvest moon shining down. I don't remember if the street was as noisy as the diner had been since I was busy concentrating on the girl next to me who was holding my hand and resting her head gently against my shoulder. As we rounded the corner onto a quiet side street, she asked me to kiss her. Well, you didn't have to hit this Marine over the head. I gave her a short kiss directly on her lips and then stood back and smiled.

23

"Is that the best you can do, Marine?"

Before I could respond, she planted one on me that must have lasted for several minutes at least. I held her as tightly as I could without crushing her ribs. Her breasts felt heavenly against my chest. I couldn't believe that this was really happening to me . . . shy Jim Mathews . . . the one who never had had a girlfriend all during high school. I had dated a few girls back home, but somehow never hit it off with any of them. Part of it was due to the stigma of my mother's affair and part of it because I needed to work and just didn't have the time to get involved with women and spend money that I really didn't have to throw away.

Stupidly, I suggested that maybe we should get back to Bob and Betty . . . I wasn't sure how either of them would take being alone together. Helen agreed. We decided against seeing a movie since it was obvious Betty didn't find Bob exciting at all and vice versa.

"But I hope we can get together again tomorrow before you have to leave?"

"I think the bus leaves at five. I'll check on it and call you in the morning. Will you be at the boarding house, or do you go to church on Sunday morning?"

"I'll skip church tomorrow if you promise you'll call and let us get together before you have to go. Pasquales has a wonderful Sunday brunch."

"Then it's a date.

Now, we'd better check on Betty and Bob."

Maria paused the VCR.

"Mom, you never told me about how you and Dad met. Is that story true?"

Helen paused for several moments, not wanting to interrupt her reverie.

"Yes, that's pretty much how it all happened. I knew he was the one for me the minute I laid eyes on him. The day after we met, I must confess I thought he wasn't going to call. I waited at the boarding house all day and was relieved when his call came.

Just think where you'd be if he hadn't called."

Maria smiled.

"Are you ready to resume the story?"

"Yes. Please."

CHAPTER FIVE

I didn't know it at the time, but that Sunday afternoon in Washington would be the last time I would see Helen for a very long time. However, those unforeseen and unexpected hours together were enough to seal a relationship that would last a lifetime. We kept the day simple: a casual walk on the national mall followed by a stop at the Lincoln memorial; then lunch at a small sidewalk café on Pennsylvania Avenue a few blocks from the White House. We decided that would be more intimate than Pasquales. They were always crowded at Sunday brunch. Then we took a slow romantic walk back to where I was to meet Bob for the bus trip back to the base.

Bob had done the noble thing and taken Betty to lunch; but I think he had made it abundantly clear to her that while he found her company pleasant, there was no spark between them such as was obvious between Helen and me. It would undoubtedly be their last time together. Helen held me tightly as the bus approached and we each vowed that we would write as soon as possible. As the bus pulled away from the curb in front of the Y.M.C.A., I was sure I saw a tear in Helen's eye . . . and I felt as though I could cry as well. I hadn't felt such angst at a departure in quite some time . . . probably not since I had left my mother under similar circumstances the day I boarded the bus for Parris Island and then when I said goodbye to her when I was leaving for Quantico.

Often, when I thought back on those days during my many lonely moments during the war, I couldn't help but wonder what power in the universe had preordained the two of us to meet so randomly . . . and what power kept me safe so that I could return to her when the war was over. I wonder too what force kept the two of us so dedicated to each other that she would be waiting for me when at last I returned from those dreadful years overseas.

The day after Bob and I returned to Quantico, I was told that as soon as my training was done there, I would be returning to Parris Island as an associate instructor. Apparently I had done something right during boot camp and infantry training as well. I had only been a private first class for a few months, but I would proceed there with the rank of sergeant. And if things went well, I could expect another promotion within a short time. It was another sign of things heating up in the world.

The pall of impending war in this country had the military in an uneasy frame of mind. Hitler had been invading numerous countries in Europe; England was now involved and it was clear that Churchill wanted the help of the American people. He had made that abundantly clear to President Roosevelt. It was anyone's guess as to how long he could stall our entry into the fray. There were many who felt it was none of our business, but still others with keen foresight who knew and understood that the dawning era of globalism could not keep us out of it.

I was pleasantly surprised when only a few days after returning to Quantico, I received a lovely note from Helen. It was quite warm and friendly and I could sense that she was hoping to hear from me and get my thoughts on our brief but romantic time in Washington. So, I sat down as soon as I could and sent her the most endearing thoughts that had been on my mind since the bus pulled away from the curb leaving her standing there looking forlorn. I wanted to let her know in no uncertain terms that our meeting had been more than just a casual affair for me and that I had every intention of making good on my promise to keep in touch by mail, by phone, and whenever possible in person.

The only uncertainty lay in the fact that I wasn't sure where the corps might send me and when. Infantry trained people like myself wouldn't stay as drill instructors forever. In the event that war broke out . . . and that was looking more probable with each passing day . . . and if I were sent into battle . . . equally likely . . . would I survive combat?

She quickly answered my letter and confirmed her feelings for me, making me feel wanted . . . something every G.I. needs when facing the uncertainties of war.

There was no time for another trip to D.C. before my departure for South Carolina, so I suggested that perhaps she should consider coming there to visit me. I knew it was a bit risqué suggesting such a thing in those days . . . but she agreed unhesitatingly. And so it only remained for me to get my schedule after my arrival back at Parris Island and make the necessary arrangements.

Nineteen forty segued into ninety forty-one and the threat of war continued to escalate around the world. Various nations were forming alliances against each other and it was evident that a new world war was about to be thrust upon the globe.

We continued to churn out recruits in the remarkably short period of only six weeks. Most of the recruits were remarkably dedicated to the cause of keeping world peace and gave their all to the learning process set forth by the corps at Parris Island. Having been a recent graduate of the program, I was impressed at the caliber of Marines that we were turning out. But at the same time, I was painfully aware of their inexperience in actual combat . . . as I was of my own . . . and I knew that if and when we were brought into the conflict . . . as surely we would be . . . that many of them would not survive for long once the shooting began. I considered my own mortality each time I looked at a new crop of raw recruits step off the bus at the processing center.

It was early March before I could see my way clear to invite Helen to come to South Carolina. She arranged to leave on a Thursday by bus. With all the stops and transfers necessary, she wouldn't arrive in Beaufort (the nearest town to Parris Island) until late Friday night. I made arrangements for her to stay at a small inn there.

❧

The minute she stepped off the bus, dressed in a gingham dress with a shawl draped over her shoulders, I was immediately brought back to what had attracted to me when I first set eyes on her that fateful evening in Washington several months earlier. She approached me with a familiarity that let me know that our meeting would be a continuation of our initial encounter together. There was no need for a warm up, no need to act like strangers getting reacquainted. The sense of belonging was immediate and she was keenly aware that I felt it too.

We kissed briefly at the station but held back showing our deeper emotions until I had her safely ensconced in her room at the inn. There, I shared with her how I had missed every moment we had been apart and had counted the days and hours until her arrival. She said that she had felt exactly the same way and had even counted minutes that we were not together. We practically fell onto the bed together once in the room and kissed and hugged and shared moments about our life apart since our last meeting.

"I've only shared these feelings with one other person . . . Betty. She could tell from the way we acted around one another that our relationship was destined to be serious."

"And how is Betty? Did she ever hear any more from Bob?"

Helen cast a disapproving glance my way.

"Now I think you already know the answer to that question."

"Yes, I suppose I do. But you have to understand that I haven't seen or heard from Bob since I left Quantico for here. I knew he hadn't said anything more about her after we returned from Washington in October."

"But, she has been seeing a sailor quite regularly for the past several months. He works at the Navy Department and I think she is very serious about him; I know that he likes her.

So, we'll just have to see how it goes."

"Now" I interjected, "I'll bet you're starved."

"Well, now that you mention it, I haven't had much to eat. The last I had was some fruit I bought at the bus stop in Charleston. I must say that it appears to be a very quaint town from what I could see of it. The rivers you have to cross getting here are very beautiful. But what I liked best of all was the real Southern accent of the colored folks that ran the fruit stand at the bus depot.

Why, I could barely understand a word they spoke. It's nothing like where I come from."

I suddenly realized that I didn't know a thing about Helen's past . . . where she was born or what her parents did or how and why she came to be in Washington, D.C.

She told me that she had been raised in a town in central Connecticut . . . the same as Betty . . . and had come to Washington along with her boss, the former mayor of the town. He had assumed a position in one of the newly created federal agencies in the Roosevelt administration and Helen was his executive secretary.

"It's a long story.

I got sick during my eighth grade year in Catholic school. Since I had to stay out almost the entire year, it would have meant that I would have to repeat the grade and be left behind from all my friends.

I didn't want that.

So I enrolled in business school instead and became a secretary. I'm good at what I do and I was quickly promoted to assistant to the mayor . . . and you know the rest of the story . . . except that he is thinking about running for the United States Senate next year. Our senior senator just announced that he plans to retire at the end of his current term, so it leaves that race wide open. He apparently just found out that he is terminally ill . . . so there was no time for him to groom anyone for his position.

By the way, my parents came to the U.S. from Italy . . . from two small towns not far from Naples. The original family name was Brandisi, but my father left off the 'isi' when he registered at Ellis Island. Many people from different countries did that to make their names sound more American and less ethnic.

My father has his own barber shop back home and my mother takes care of our house and the rest of the family. I have two brothers and two sisters all of whom live and work there as well."

"Does the town have a name?" I enquired. I always was a stickler for details.

"Of course, silly. It's Meriden."

Already I was liking her familiarity with me.

"And what about the towns in Italy where your parents came from?"

"My, you do like a lot of detail.

Well, my father came from a tiny town called Campagna and my mother from a nearby town called Eboli. They're both in Salerno province in the region called Campania. Naples, which is approximately fifty miles away, is the capital of the region."

"Were they married before they came to America?"

"No.

That's the funny part. Their hometowns are about five miles apart, but they never met until they arrived in America and were living in New York City of all places. After a few years there, they married and then moved to Connecticut and started a family.

I'm the youngest of the five."

"I'm afraid I'm an only child."

"Most of my family works for or has worked for International Silver Company in Meriden. They're one of the largest silver manufacturing companies in America. My sister Theresa and my brother Tony work there now. And my sister Eva now works for a company that makes display cases for International.

My oldest brother Mike is a piano teacher. And Tony plays the piano and the violin.

I'm afraid the girls have no musical talent."

"Well, you're right at home with me and my family. I don't remember anyone so much as playing a harmonica at my house. The closest I ever came to playing music was tapping my shoes against the church pew while the organist played and the choir sang at church services."

Helen smiled and warmly squeezed my hand.

I leaned into her and kissed her softly on the lips.

"Say, did I ever tell you that I think I'm in love with you?"

She forced a smile, while tears were forming at the corners of her eyes.

"Oh, God.

I so wanted to hear you say that. I felt guilty coming all the way down here without some assurance about your feelings for me . . . but now you've given that to me. I wanted to tell you that I loved you too back in Washington . . . but I was afraid you'd think I was rushing things."

I held her in my arms and gently stroked her hair.

"I was afraid you'd think I was only after one thing if I moved too fast . . . but I had this feeling of being comfortable with you from the moment we met. I'd never felt that way about anyone before."

She savored the moment in my arms.

"I had the same feelings, but I didn't know exactly how to phrase it . . . you've said it so beautifully."

She elevated her mouth toward mine and together we shared a lingering kiss. I still had reservations about taking things any farther physically, so I jumped up and said:

"And now, let's get you something to eat."

CHAPTER SIX

Helen hadn't ever quite gotten used to southern cooking though it was frequent fare at the boarding house. Alongside the fried chicken were plentiful helpings of collard greens and black eyed peas; and in a basket in the center of the table, corn bread and biscuits. And off to the side was a small tub of butter.

"My! You southerners sure know how to fatten a girl up."

"Well, of course, you don't have to eat it all" I said with tongue in cheek and a smile on my face.

"I wouldn't want to be impolite to my host" she replied in kind.

I reached for her hand under the table and gave it a tight squeeze.

"Would you like some more iced tea?"

"Goodness no. I believe there is enough sugar in there to bake a cake. Maybe just a cup of coffee."

"We like our sugar with a little tea flavor down here" I laughed in response.

I motioned for the waitress and ordered two cups of coffee. As we sat and talked about nothing in particular, I was startled to see two MPs enter the small restaurant. One of them walked up to the counter area and spoke to the owner. Then he turned and spoke to all the patrons.

"Parris Island has just been placed on full alert. All passes and leaves have been cancelled. Anyone here on active duty needs to report to his unit right away."

The pair then exited the building. Numerous men seated at tables immediately stood and hastily made their way to the door.

Helen looked at me.

"What does that mean?" she asked softly.

"I'm afraid my dear that it means our weekend together has most likely just been wrecked. I won't know for sure what is going on until I report to the base. So, I'm going to have to take you back to the inn and get to my unit. Sometimes these are just readiness alerts, meaning they just want to see how long it takes to round everyone up in the case of a real emergency."

I motioned to the waitress for the check.

Helen already had tears in her eyes at the thought that her eagerly anticipated trip to South Carolina might have been wasted, but more importantly she was concerned that if it were real I might be heading for danger.

I did my best to assuage her fears.

Within fifteen minutes, I had her back at the inn.

"I just want to remind you that I love you and I don't want you to be worrying about me. I can take care of myself. If you need anything, the innkeeper will help you. I'll try to get word back to you as soon as I can about the situation. As I said earlier, hopefully it's just a drill."

I wiped the tears from her eyes as I prepared to leave.

"Jim I love you too. Now you take care of yourself and let me hear from you as soon as you can. Meanwhile, I'll just be waiting for your return."

I held her tight and kissed her quickly, albeit passionately.

"Now, I really must go."

I turned quickly and left the room.

"Oh damn" was all she could say as she flung herself onto the bed.

At the base, things were in their usual state of orderly chaos that I was now quite familiar with. Being a training facility, things were not quite the same as a base housing a regular mobile division.

The staff had been prepared for news of actual war and how they were to respond. Any recruits more than half way through basic training were *immediately to be transferred to active status and readied for deployment. If they were less than half way, they were to be put into an indefinite hold situation at Parris Island until matters were clarified at the most senior levels of command.*

I entered my command post only to find out that this was to be a weeklong readiness drill. The staff and appropriately trained recruits (more than half way) were to be deployed to the brand new amphibious training facility near Jacksonville, North Carolina, about three hundred and fifty miles to the north.

Apparently plans had been under way for some time for the exercise since troop transport provisions were awaiting the off duty staff's arrival. The duty personnel and recruits were already standing by.

"Sergeant Mathews, you are hereby promoted to the temporary rank of Gunnery Sergeant and will be in charge of all the recruits from our barracks and the two adjoining barracks as well."

I stared at my company commander, Captain John Meyer, somewhat in disbelief at what I had just heard.

"Gunny, did you hear what I just said?"

I immediately turned full face to Captain Meyer and saluted crisply.

"Sir!

Yes sir!

And thank you sir for your confidence in me."

"You've earned it.

And now, we need to get moving as soon as possible. We're supposed to be in North Carolina by this time tomorrow."

"Sir, if I may ask a favor?" I explained my predicament to the captain.

"You have one hour to make arrangements for your girl to return to Washington and to get yourself back here. I wish I could make it more."

He smiled.

"It's been a long time since I was first in love, Gunny."

"Thank you, sir."

I was back at the inn within ten minutes and immediately broke the bad news to Helen. She hung on my every word as I explained that it would be best if I arranged for her transportation back to Washington the next morning. As I spoke, she began to cry.

"Unfortunately, this is only a sample of what it will be like to be part of a military family. Hopefully I'll be back here within a week, but it's not unusual for plans to change. And if war does break out, needless to say I could be gone for months or even years."

"Does this mean that you're thinking of making me part of your family? If so, then I'll do whatever you ask of me."

I was caught slightly off guard. Although thoughts of marriage had entered my mind, I wasn't quite prepared to make that commitment yet.

"Can we discuss that when I get back . . . I don't want to rush such an important decision?"

She smiled and clung to me, taking that as a positive answer.

I raised her chin and kissed her deeply.

"Now, I have to get back to the base. But I'll stop at the desk and ask the inn keeper to arrange for your bus ticket home. I'll get in touch with you just as soon as I can. And you write me every day . . . I want a whole stack of letters waiting for me when I get back."

She assured me that she would and with that I was gone.

CHAPTER SEVEN

The innkeeper kindly arranged Helen's passage back to Washington, D.C. on the following day's only bus that departed promptly at ten a.m. Like the trip to South Carolina, it made stops at several places, albeit different ones. After Columbia came Charlotte, North Carolina and then Raleigh, the capital city. There she changed buses and made additional stops in Rocky Mount, North Carolina and Richmond, Virginia before arriving home the following day at about three p.m.

Helen was tired by the time she finally made it to her room, but mostly she was disappointed at the events that had separated her from her man . . . that's how she now thought of me.

Her man.

It had an appealing ring to it and made her feel all tingly way down deep inside her most womanly parts. She had wept silently most of the trip, fearing that something might happen to me; but she remembered the reassuring words that I had spoken just before departing:

"I can take care of myself."

Then she thought about my final words . . . to write every day, so she immediately sat down and began to compose the first of those daily missives.

I returned to the base precisely one hour after being given permission to leave, and already the deployment was in full gear. I quickly grabbed my helmet and travel gear already stuffed into a duffel bag and proceeded to the designated rally point.

"Gunny, we're just about ready to shove off. If you'll be so kind as to give the word."

I almost turned to see if someone else was behind me, when I realized that I was the one being addressed. The corporal approached me and handed me a small package.

"The captain asked me to give you these."

I opened the bag and found a pair of gunnery sergeant's stripes inside, along with two safety pins.

"The captain said you can get them sewed on later."

I nodded my thanks.

"Let me just check with the formation leader."

Back in a few minutes, I barked out to the corporal:

"We're to follow the set of trucks just ahead of us there and they should be moving out in about five minutes. So everyone get in their places and standby."

He affirmed the order and passed the word to the other men in the company. Within ten minutes we were on our way to North Carolina.

My only previous visits to North Carolina occurred while traversing the state to and from Quantico. I had never been near the coastal areas although I assumed they would be similar to those around Parris Island.

The weather en route had been dismal. It was like the spring monsoons I had heard about in some foreign countries. Those in the know had said it was distinctly unusual to see that much rain during the spring months . . . although not unheard of. Several times we were forced to pull off the road because of the torrents of rain being blown so hard that visibility was reduced to zero.

We used the coastal route US 17 that ran all the way from near Parris Island through South Carolina and into North Carolina just south of Wilmington and then northward to our destination. The roads in that *era were still primitive. Numerous large "potholes" made travel dangerous. When hit at high speed, they could take out a tire and inner tube instantly and throw a vehicle into an uncontrollable rollover. Fortunately, the convoy leader hadn't allowed that to happen, slowing to a crawl whenever he felt it necessary. Many of the soldiers in the trailing vehicles accused him of not knowing how to drive since they felt we were going much too slowly . . . but they were neither in charge nor responsible for the lives of the troops.*

As we left the "low country" as the area around Beaufort was called, the terrain changed dramatically and not for the better. Gone were the beautiful large oak trees hung with Spanish moss. Instead, there were only small scrub brush blown by the winds along the shore; and increasing numbers of sand dunes.

By the following day, we approached the small town of Jacksonville, adjacent to the area being developed into the amphibious training facility and set up our gear for the duration of the exercise.

Helen was kept busy by her job, but she remained anxious awaiting news that "her man" was safe. She knew that there would be days . . . or perhaps weeks . . . with no communication from me. She wasn't sure if there was any way for her letters to reach me until my safe return from whatever it was she thought I was doing. I had made it abundantly clear to her that much of my business was necessarily kept secret from the public. The nation was anxious about events taking place in other parts of the world and somewhat paranoid about the possible presence of spies operating in the country. The military had been instructed accordingly.

My men and I along with the other participants in the exercise had set up our tent city and prepared for the planned amphibious exercises that were being developed at the fresh site along the New River. The base did not have a formal name as yet and was simply called Marine Barracks, New River. Eventually, it would come to be known as Camp LeJeune. The base headquarters had been set up in an old cottage on Montford Point and the rest of the facility was in various phases of construction.

"Gunny, I want you to take your men along with two other squads to the ocean front where we have some craft that are being developed for beach landings. Some guy named Higgins has been working on a design for the corps for some time that combines a large boat with a Japanese designed

hinged bow-ramp. They hold about thirty-six men. When they approach the beach, the bow opens and provides a platform to exit the craft onto the sand.

I'm curious to see it myself."

"Yes, sir!"

"And Jim" Captain Meyer added less formally, "be careful and make sure all your men can swim. We don't want any training fatalities."

As soon as he was gone, I turned to my men.

"Saddle up, men, and follow me."

We all stood and surveyed the newly configured Higgins boats and scratched our heads figuratively.

"Gunny, just what in God's name do they expect us to do in those things? Do we jump over the side when we reach our destination?

And just how fast can a boat go when the front end is squared off like that?" the corporal asked me while pointing at the front of the Higgins boat.

All fair questions I thought to myself.

"Well, if I understand it right, that front end opens up making a platform to exit onto the beach. You all stay here while I check our schedule with the beach master."

The men could see me conversing with the sergeant in charge of the exercise. When I returned a few minutes later, I addressed them.

"We're to form up behind those other men over there. Then we'll be divided up into groups of about thirty-five for each boat. They'll take us a few hundred yards off shore and then turn around and make a run at the beach. There'll be a platoon stationed on the beach firing live ammo over our heads to simulate a real landing.

So I want you all to treat this like the real thing. And for God's sake, keep your heads down. I don't want someone getting killed just because he forgot to stay low during the beach assault.

Do you hear me?" I bellowed, reminiscent of Drill Sergeant Anderson.

They answered much as we had in boot camp.

"Yes sir, Gunny Mathews."

Smiling, I acknowledged the cohesiveness of the group and their willingness to follow my every command without question.

"Now, form up.

Double time it."

The men broke into a run and queued up behind the others already in line.

∽

The grueling training at Parris Island had not quite prepared us for the amphibious assault exercises we now found ourselves participating in. The weather had been rough thanks to an early spring storm that had churned up the Atlantic all along coastal North Carolina. Coming from Arkansas, I hadn't earned my sea legs . . . in fact, except for fishing once in a small boat on a tiny lake back home, I had never been on the water at all . . . certainly nothing like the large expanse of Atlantic Ocean that we now faced.

As our boat bucked the incoming waves, many of my men became seasick immediately and vomited on the deck of the craft. I had all I could do to contain myself and thought that at any minute I might join them. As the boat passed the breakwater and the sea smoothed out, most everyone settled down as the craft made its way to the turnaround point several hundred yards out. Then as they reversed course and made their way back towards shore, things became unsettled again.

"Alright men, prepare to disembark.

When you hear the ship's driver give the warning, we'll have thirty seconds to landing. When the ramp opens, be prepared to exit immediately. Keep low and make your way onto the open beach. Try to find anything you can to stay behind for protection.

Remember, there will be live firing going on over your heads. Keep in mind that in a real combat situation the enemy will be firing directly at you trying to kill you. So speed is the key to reaching your objective and staying alive!

Any questions?"

I found them all a little anxious, but no one spoke.

"Good.

I'll see you on the beach."

∽

Ten Higgins craft made a staged approach to the beach, five at a time each parallel to the other. As they approached the breakwater, things became chaotic as the waves pitched the boats unmercifully. Most of the men became sick once again.

40

Just then the driver gave the thirty seconds warning.

"O.K. men.

This is it. Grab your Garands and follow me."

The boat made a sudden stop as it hit the sand; the doors exploded open and we were exposed immediately. Sounds of bullets whistling over our heads caught our attention and reminded us of the seriousness of our mission and the urgency in disembarking and making for the beach as expeditiously as possible.

I could see some barricades that had been erected on the beach to provide some cover during the run to our objective.

"We'll rendezvous on the north end of the barricade" I yelled as we hit the sand running in a semi-crouched position. My men followed me in similar fashion until the boat was emptied and the driver reversed engines and took the craft back out to sea to make way for the second wave waiting immediately behind them.

The mock enemy continued firing at us as we hurried to the rendezvous point. Suddenly there was the sound of one of my men crying out in agony.

"I've been hit! I've been hit."

When I looked around, I could see one of my men lying face up on the sand holding his thigh tightly. I signaled to the squad corpsman to see to the man and report his findings to me as soon as he could. I returned my attention to the work at hand as we gathered together before our final assault on the objective that lay some hundred or more yards inland. It was a bunker that had been built into a sand dune and was the site for the gunners that had been firing over our heads during the landing.

The corpsman quickly arrived at the site and reported that the injured Marine only had a flesh wound that apparently had been caused by a ricocheting round that must have hit something firm at the water's edge.

"Good. Can he walk?"

"He'll need someone to help support him."

"Then just make him comfortable until our objective is secured."

"Yes, Gunny."

It took almost two hours for me and my squad to secure our objective. It was necessary for us to fan out and approach it from all sides in order to divert attention from the gun placements.

When I finally stood together with my men at the objective and declared "victory", we all gave a sigh of relief. But then I quietly thought about what it must be like in real combat, with the enemy coming at you from all sides and bullets being aimed directly at you. My squad had suffered only the one minor injury from a ricocheting bullet. How many would be lying dead somewhere on the beach or in the water in actual combat? I had heard the horror stories from World War I veterans about life at the front and the untold casualties from the new weaponry introduced in that conflict; and the utter devastation to troops from the poisonous gases used in the trench warfare. As a squad leader, would I be able to accept such losses of my own men and fellow comrades? I knew it was a problem that all leaders in battle must eventually face and come to grips with.

"Great job men!" I said to the assembled squad.

"Now, let's get to the chow line. We've got another beach assault planned for this afternoon."

I heard a few groans from the squad members, but chose to ignore them as they had done well in my estimation on our first amphibious training exercise.

CHAPTER EIGHT

My squad and I were elated when they announced mail call during meal break between the assault exercises. I was especially thrilled when the corporal distributing the mail handed me a letter postmarked Washington, D.C. and bearing Helen's return address.

I stole away from the group to read it. Helen's words were for my eyes only; I didn't want any inquisitive neighbors asking who was writing to me or what they had to say.

I treasured my privacy.

> *"My darling Jim,*
>
> > *I hope that you are safe wherever this letter finds you. I pray that you are not in any danger.*
> >
> > *I want you to know how very much I miss you. I made it back to Washington without any trouble after the gentleman at the Inn made the arrangements for me. I was sad the whole way back, however, at not being able to spend the time together that we had planned. But I know that we can make up for that as soon as you are able to get leave. I try to stay busy at work so that*

I am not worrying about you all the time . . . but it is hard not to think about your gentleness and loving ways.

Please write when you can. I will understand if I don't hear from you as I know you and your men are training for a war all of us hope will never come . . . but if it does, we certainly want you and our country to be prepared for it.

Know that I love you and please stay safe."

Love,

Helen

Her words almost made me cry. She told me about her after work activities that included going to church and an occasional movie with Betty and her new boyfriend as well as writing to me. As I sat by myself and reminisced over the letter's contents, I was suddenly startled by one of my men.

"Sergeant, the captain would like to see you."

"Thank you, corporal."

"Sergeant Mathews reporting as ordered, sir" I said crisply saluting Captain Meyer.

"At ease, Gunny.

You and your men did a fine job for a first time assault using brand new equipment. I see that you had one injury. Was it serious?"

"No sir. Just a flesh wound to the leg. The corpsman took care of it in the field and we have him being tended to by our surgeon. He thinks the corporal . . . John Miller . . . will be able to resume duty in a day or two.

Apparently it resulted from a ricocheting bullet that struck some of the metal along the beach."

"Good.

What I wanted to see you about concerns selecting someone from this unit to be assigned to Officers Candidate School. I've had my eye on you for some time as have several of the more senior officers in the division. All of us can't help but notice that you have a way with your men that indicates real leadership potential. Your records indicate that you were a platoon corporal at Parris Island and quickly advanced to the rank of sergeant after infantry training.

How would you like to go back to Quantico for OCS? You'd be a second lieutenant in about ten weeks. There is a new class starting right after Labor Day, so you'd be finished by Thanksgiving.

Now, if you need some time to think about it, take whatever you need."

"No sir.

"You see, I have a girl in D.C., so that would be perfect. It would give me a chance to see her more often."

"Mathews, I hope that's not the only reason you're saying yes to my proposal."

"No sir.

I love the corps, sir and my intentions were always to become an officer."

"Good.

Then it's decided. I'll submit your name as soon as we get back to Parris Island. It should be a mere formality.

And gunny, mum's the word about this for now."

"Yes sir."

With that tucked under my hat, I headed back to my men.

The second assault landing went off without a hitch. My squad reached our objective in half the time as the first and there were no casualties. The good news of the day was that we were to repeat the exercise once daily for three more days, then return to Parris Island where we would be given a three day weekend pass.

Of course, I immediately dashed off a letter to Helen asking if she could arrange another trip to South Carolina for that weekend.

When we arrived back in South Carolina, I had my answer waiting. It was Wednesday and Helen would arrive late Friday afternoon. I made arrangements for her again at the inn and bided my time until I could hold her again and tell her the good news . . . I had received official notification of selection for OCS school in Quantico beginning in September, 1941.

I hoped . . . assumed . . . that she would be as thrilled at the news as I was, for I saw it as an opportunity for us to be together more frequently. And if things continued on their current course, plans for marriage would certainly be on the horizon as soon as I was commissioned a second lieutenant and had an adequate income to support a wife and possible family.

The whole way from Washington D.C. to Beaufort, Helen had only one thing on her mind . . . her man. The thought of seeing me and being held and caressed by me kept her mind racing throughout the almost thirty hour sojourn. She closed her eyes only a few times and even then she thought of me.

Needless to say, I too was counting the hours until the bus's arrival. I was frustrated by the fact that I wouldn't know if it was to be on time until I literally saw it pull into the station. Fortunately, the weather was good and the bus arrived right on schedule. As it pulled into its stall at the depot, I could see Helen's face through the dust covered windows of the bus. She smiled the instant she saw me and starting waving her hand feverishly. I waved as well as I made my way to the bus's door. As she approached the exit steps, she flung herself into my arms.

I stepped back from the bus, held her tightly and performed a pirouette. She giggled like a school girl.

"Put me down" she said, somewhat embarrassed in front of the crowd of passengers and others gathered about the disembarkation point. But I continued to hold her, as I proceeded to a more secluded part of the station where we embraced and kissed each other passionately.

"God I've missed you. I was so worried that something would happen and you wouldn't make it back as planned. Let's not have any sudden exits like happened the last time I came all the way down here to see you."

Smiling, I looked deeply into her eyes.

"It would take a war to get me to leave you this time. Come on, let's get your things and get you to the inn. I've got a lot of things to tell you."

She looked at me quizzically.

"Not until later," I added somewhat mysteriously.

"O.K." she answered.

"Come over here" I said just as soon as we reached her room at the inn. I sat in an overstuffed chair and patted my knee.

She sat and kissed me.

"Now, what is so important that you need to tell me?"

"Well, first of all, I've been selected to go to OCS starting sometime around Labor Day. My company commander, Captain Meyer, submitted my name and assured me it would be a mere formality . . . and it was. I should have my orders any day now."

My comments obviously didn't register with her.

"What is OCS?"

"I'm sorry . . . that stands for Officer Candidate School. And to answer your next question . . . her face lit up at the thought that indeed I was reading her mind . . . it means that when I finish the school sometime around Thanksgiving, I'll be commissioned a second lieutenant in the Marine Corps . . . an officer."

"Oh Jim, that's great."

"Wait, there's more good news. OCS is held in Quantico, so I'll be nearby D.C. during the twelve or thirteen weeks of school. And once I'm an officer, I'll be making a good salary . . . enough to support a family."

The look on Helen's face was one that I remember to this day . . . first an element of almost disbelief at what she was hearing followed by a smile that could cheer up the dreariest day imaginable.

She grabbed me around the neck and gave me a big kiss.

"Does this mean . . . ?"

"Yes.

It means that I'm asking you to wait until I finish OCS and then I want to officially ask you to marry me."

"Of course I'll wait for you . . . forever if I have to."

That line was more prophetic than she could have ever imagined when she uttered it.

"And now, my dear, I bet you could use something to eat. You've had a long trip from D.C."

CHAPTER NINE

The weekend passed by faster than either of us would have liked and Monday morning Helen was on the ten a.m. bus back to Washington.

Precisely two weeks later, I was notified by Captain Meyer that my official start date for OCS would be the day after Labor Day . . . and that I would be given ten days leave of absence prior to reporting. I was so excited that I decided to call Helen on the telephone . . . something that I had never resorted to previously in my entire life.

This was big news . . . with special implications for our future lives together. The local Post Exchange had a phone booth especially for urgent matters . . . and I felt that this definitely qualified. I had kept the number to the phone located in the parlor of Helen's boarding house since she gave it to me when we first met.

"Operator, I'd like to call Washington, D.C. The number is Dupont 3465."

Several moments passed as the operator placed the call. It had to be relayed to Columbia, South Carolina and then to Richmond, Virginia before finally ending with the Washington, D.C. operator who made the connection to the phone located in the boarding house.

"Please deposit four dollars and fifty cents for the first three minutes."

I had come prepared with ten dollars worth of quarters. After the eighteenth quarter had registered, the operator triggered the call. I could hear the phone ringing. Finally, after the seventh ring, I could hear someone on the other end.

"Mrs. Callender's boarding house. This is Mary speaking."

"My name is Sergeant Jim Mathews and I'd like to speak to Helen Brand, please. I'm calling long distance." I hoped that bit of news would hurry her along in getting Helen to the phone.

I could hear a giggle on the other end. I assumed that Helen must have mentioned my name to her . . . and undoubtedly something about the nature of our relationship.

"Just a minute, Sergeant. She's upstairs in her room. I'll get her for you."

I could hear the minutes ticking off in my brain. Money wasn't the most important thing on my mind, but I was aware of the cost of the call and hoped I had enough quarters.

"Jim, is everything all right?"

Suddenly, she was there and typical of the era immediately assumed that a phone call or a telegram carried some ominous news.

"Everything is just great, my love. I just received official news that I'm to report to Quantico the day after Labor Day for the thirteen week OCS course.

And . . . . " I hesitated long enough to pique her interest.

"And I'll get ten days leave before I have to report. So I figure you and I can make some plans on just how to use those ten day together."

"Oh, Jim, that's marvelous.

How would you like to go to Connecticut and meet my family? We can also go down to the shore . . . that is if you like sunshine and salty water? And there are several amusement parks and other fun things nearby that I think you might like."

"My dear, anything you say will be just fine with me as long as we are together.

Say, just how will we get there?"

"We can take the Metro from here to New York. Then the New York, New Haven and Hartford railroad goes right through Meriden and makes stops there several times a day."

Before I could answer, the operator cut in abruptly.

"Please deposit another four dollars for three additional minutes."

Well, I plunked in the sixteen quarters and then continued.

"Now, where were we?"

"And when we get to Meriden, my brother Tony can pick us up in his car. He's got a big new Packard. I'm sure he won't mind if we use it while we're there."

"But I don't know how to drive" I added sheepishly.

"That's all right. I'll teach you" Helen boasted.

"You know how to drive a car?" I asked with an air of skepticism.

"Don't you think women are capable of doing those sorts of things?"

"Sure. I guess I just never thought about it. We didn't have a car back home."

"I guess we'd better hang up. I don't want you to spend all your spare money on one phone call. Why don't you write me with all the details and I'll make arrangements on my end to be off when you get here. And I'll let the family know to expect us toward the end of August.

Jim, I love you."

"And I love you too, my darling.

Write soon."

"I promise I will."

The impertinent operator broke in again.

"I'm hanging up right now" I said as I placed the phone back on the receiver.

I could imagine Helen smiling and sobbing at the same time. She would have liked to listen to my voice for hours, but she knew that was not possible for now.

I almost shed a tear as I was forced to end the call, but smiled as I thought of the days and years ahead with her.

✍

My current and last recruit group finished basic training and I was officially detached from Parris Island with orders to proceed to Quantico, Virginia and OCS. Formal classes would commence on Wednesday, September 3, 1941 and end on Friday, the fifth of December of the same year.

My last official day at Parris Island was Friday, August 22. I had already checked the bus and train schedules and found that I could take a train from Savannah, Georgia to Washington leaving that same evening and arriving in D.C. late the following day, Saturday. Fortunately, the Marine Corps had a bus to Savannah that would get me there in time to make the connection.

I had communicated this to Helen via a letter and she had replied that she would be waiting at Union Station when my train arrived. She closed with words of love that touched my heart. All our past loneliness would soon be a memory.

Chapter Ten

My final day with the troops at Parris Island arrived before I knew it; it was a mixed blessing for me. I had enjoyed my role teaching young men like myself the basics of combat skills and the necessity for discipline especially during the rigors of battle.

Rumors of impending war continued to circulate and preparations for that inevitability were increasing daily in the military facilities around the country and abroad.

I was sad to leave many of my comrades with whom I had served for the better part of my time in the military. They would soon be my juniors as I advanced to the officer ranks. While I was somewhat disappointed that they did not throw me a farewell party, I was equally thankful when I realized how traumatic such affairs often were, knowing I may never see many of them alive again should a world conflict erupt.

I was only too glad to board the Atlantic Coast Line train at Savannah, Georgia that would deliver me to Washington, D.C. and to Helen in a matter of hours.

cↈ

As the train pulled into Washington's Union Station, I could see literally hundreds of people waiting for their loved ones who were arriving. Among the crowd, I somehow was able to find Helen and began yelling her name as the train slowed to a halt and began discharging passengers. She heard my voice and caught a glimpse of me just as I disembarked from my car.

We ran straight for each other. As she approached, I pulled her close to me and held her tight.

"Oh, I'm so glad to see you" she said gazing into my eyes.

"My family is so anxious to meet you.

I thought we'd spend the night here in Washington and then take the eleven o'clock train to New York tomorrow morning . . . if that's all right with you?"

She smiled and leaned into my lips again and again as she spoke.

"Any thing you say or do is just fine with me, my darling."

She looked up lovingly at me.

"Say it again.

I love having you call me 'my darling'."

I looked into her eyes and kissed her softly on the lips.

"My darling."

We stood clinging to each other for a few moments and then realized that most of the crowd that had briefly surrounded us had already dispersed.

"Let me grab my things and we'll be on our way. What did you have planned for the evening?"

"First we'll get you settled in your room at the boarding house . . . one of the men there is gone for the week and said you could use his room for the night. Then I thought we'd have dinner and maybe catch a movie.

What do you think?"

"Anything you want to do is fine with me, my darling . . . as long as we're together."

"Oh, I can't wait to be Mrs. Jim Mathews."

We kissed again and then made our way to the cab stand.

We were at the train station by ten the following morning.

"I'll get the tickets since I'm familiar with the route. You get us some coffee and a table over there" she said pointing at the small café within the stations spacious assembly area.

I saluted an acknowledgement to her.

Our train had just arrived on track twenty-four from Richmond and was due to depart on time for Baltimore, Philadelphia and New York. At New York's Penn station, we would transfer to the New York, New Haven and Hartford line for the remaining ninety mile trip to Meriden. Because of our late arrival time in New York City, we would have to spend a good portion of the night in the terminal and then take the seven a.m. train to Connecticut, arriving there just before noon.

"We can just sit and talk while we wait for the next train" Helen volunteered enthusiastically after telling me our timetable to her home.

"Spending time with you is and always will be my greatest pleasure."

"You're so sweet" she cooed as I watched her sipping her coffee. She cocked her ear at an overhead announcement.

"They're announcing that our train is now boarding."

I took her hand and together we walked towards track twenty-four. After helping her up the step from the platform onto the coach, we took our seats and prepared for the first leg of our trip to Connecticut.

"I must say that these seats are much more comfortable than the ones on the train from Savannah to here. And the company is certainly much more enjoyable."

I squeezed her hand and turned and lightly kissed her.

"Well, we're off on our first big journey together. My parents and my brother Tony will be at the station to pick us up in his Packard."

"I've never owned a car, but I hear Packards are quite nice. Someday we'll own a car and you can help me pick it out."

"I'd like that."

We continued to talk about random subjects when the car suddenly lurched forward.

"Well, here we go."

Time passed quickly in Helen's presence and before we knew it we were in New York. There we sat and talked about nothing and everything and soon our train to Helen's home announced boarding.

After stops in Greenwich, Stamford, Darien, Norwalk, Bridgeport, and New Haven, our destination was finally at hand. Only one more brief stop in Wallingford and then Meriden. I could see Helen starting to fidget as we neared her home town. While she was excited to see her family once again after almost nine months away, mostly she was eager to judge their reaction to me. She had every intention of becoming my wife, with or without their approval, but she would prefer that they endorse the union.

The train began to slow as it entered Meriden's outer boundary and ahead at the station amidst the crowds of people assembled on the platform she pointed to her family so that I could get a glimpse of them before our formal meeting. As the train eased to a stop, Helen bound down the steps of the rail car and into the arms of her brother who always greeted her with a big hug and a kiss. Off to the side stood her parents.

I followed behind her quietly until she turned, grabbed my hand and said to her family: "This is my Jim."

In turn, she introduced me to her father, Felix, her mother Mary, and her brother Tony.

"Pleased to meet you, sir" I said as I shook her father's hand. Mary gave me a cursory hug but neither spoke. Tony shook my hand enthusiastically and gave me a warm verbal greeting but then deferred to Helen.

She quickly broke the silence.

"My parents don't speak English very well" she uttered looking at me. Then she turned to the whole group.

"Well, I suppose we should get on home. I'm sure we have lots to talk about."

Upon leaving the station and crossing the railroad tracks, there was a three-way intersection with a policeman controlling traffic from an elevated tower. Main Street was quaint with businesses interspersed with small open air news and fruit stands. We made the turn onto her street, Lewis Avenue.

"That's our church there", she said pointing to St. Joseph's on the corner.

One block down, Tony negotiated the Packard around the corner, onto the side street that paralleled the house. He pulled up next to the wrought iron fence gate that led to the back porch steps.

"Well, here we are!"

The three story home was awesome.

"We never had big houses like this back in Arkansas where I came from" I said to anyone listening.

"My other brother, Mike, and his family live upstairs. We live on the first floor only. The house looks bigger than it really is because of the attic and basement."

Once up the steps, we entered a small hallway that led into the kitchen on the main floor, and additional steps up to her brother's abode. We spilled into the kitchen towing our bags.

"Well, here we are."

Helen's sisters were waiting anxiously in the kitchen to meet their prospective brother-in-law.

"This is my sister Theresa" she said referring to the older looking one, "and my other sister Eva."

I extended my hand to each in turn.

"My, you and Helen look alike" I said to Theresa. Their size and features were very similar. Eva by contrast was more robust looking, with lighter hair and coarser features. She appeared to be younger than Theresa.

"We'll meet Mike and his family later. He's giving a piano lesson right now and should be home in an hour or two."

Tony announced that he was expected at home. He told Helen that he and his wife, Eddis, would expect us for dinner one day while we were visiting and that they would arrange that later. After his departure, Mary quickly put on an apron and said to me: "You must be hungry!" . . . a refrain that I would hear over and over again throughout the visit . . . in broken English.

"You never mentioned that your parents didn't speak much English." I was somewhat perturbed that so much of the conversation around me was being carried on in Italian.

"Many folks from the old country just never learn to speak English, or they speak it poorly. There are mostly Italians living here on Lewis Avenue so they continue to speak to each other in their native tongue. My brothers and sisters and I were schooled right here so we speak English all the time. I'm the only one who doesn't speak Italian well. Since I left home, I'm rarely around anyone speaking it in Washington.

But, I still understand it pretty well. And don't worry . . . they're not speaking ill of you. The only things they've said about you have been good."

That made me smile.

"Your father is especially quiet."

"He's made little effort to learn the language since his clientele at the barber shop is almost exclusively Italian men. They seem to like to keep it

that way . . . and it's good for business. But he does speak in broken English to me when I'm here. Also, he's kind of shy. I don't hear him saying much at home when I'm here. Sometimes he talks to my brothers, but he doesn't say much to us girls.

Give him a little time and he'll probably come around."

∽

I was sitting in the living room by myself while the ladies were busy in the kitchen making dinner when Helen's father appeared in the doorway. He was a small man with typical Italian features: an aquiline or Roman nose, medium dark skin and partially receding hairline. He cautiously sat down opposite me.

"I no speak good English" he uttered sheepishly. "You are soldier, no?"

I was taken aback by his approach, since I was certain from all that I had heard about Felix that such a conversation would be utterly impossible. I smiled at him.

"Yes. I am a United States Marine. I was stationed at the recruit depot at Parris Island, South Carolina until two days ago.

Now I'm on my way to becoming an officer. I have to report to the Officer Candidate School at Quantico, Virginia on September 3."

"This is good" Felix replied.

"I was soldier in Italian militia for two years before coming to America."

Well, that came as a complete surprise to me.

"What did you do in the militia?"

"I was shoe cobbler.

I never fight in war."

I never realized that there was such a position in the military, but considering that Felix's time in the militia would have been in the nineteenth century before the era of readymade foot gear, I rationalized the information.

"Just be glad that you didn't.

I've been instructing new recruits in combat techniques. It appears that we may soon be at war whether we like it or not. Mr. Roosevelt has been trying to keep us out of it, but word is that our getting into it is inevitable. We already have some troops and pilots in England at the request of Prime Minister Churchill."

"You know lot about the world."

"I try to keep up with world events since it will likely involve me sooner or later."

Felix smiled and sat quietly for a few moments. Helen appeared at the door and smiled too when she saw her father sitting with me.

"Dinner is ready."

We all made our way to the dining room where I was in for a real treat: my first authentic home cooked Italian meal: spaghetti and meatballs and a delicious dish made with rolled steak flavored with garlic and other Mediterranean herbs and spices called braciola.

My vacation time was sadly slipping away all too quickly. Helen had been a great hostess and with the help of her brother and his shiny Packard had chauffeured me around the quaint state of Connecticut. We took a swim in the now cooling waters of Long Island Sound at Hammonasset State Park beach near New Haven; enjoyed the exciting rides of two amusement parks at Savin Rock in West Haven and Lake Compounce near Bristol. And then explored Hartford, the state capital, where one of its premier attractions is the Mark Twain house where the author and his family lived from eighteen seventy-four until eighteen ninety-one.

I was treated to foods I had never seen or barely heard of in rural Arkansas such as real Italian brick oven pizza, Italian ice and a variety of pasta dishes.

When alone, we were forced to face reality. Things in Europe were continuing to deteriorate and my fear of going to war loomed large in my mind and Helen's.

"Would they take you out of OCS and send you to war?"

"I don't think so. In the first place, if war breaks out it takes a fair amount of time to ready troops and supplies for combat. And most importantly, they'll need officers . . . especially ones like me with some previous experience . . . to lead the troops in combat.

So I think I'm safe at least until after Thanksgiving this year."

Helen had a worrisome look on her face. She loved me and didn't want anything bad to happen to me. She was admittedly selfish when it came to me . . . she wanted me all for herself and the rest of the world be damned. But she knew all too well that that wasn't reality. And she knew that she had to do her patriotic duty and make sacrifices as everyone else would be called upon to do.

Our last weekend together was fast approaching and we walked downtown to the train station to check on schedules for the following Monday morning, September 1, 1941. The ten a.m. would take us to New York. There we would change trains to Washington and then I would be able to take a military bus from Marine Corps headquarters to Quantico. That same bus made daily round trips between the two so it would also be my ride to Washington on any free weekends while in school.

Helen's brother Mike lived upstairs with his wife and one son. He had done odd jobs over the years, but his current occupation was piano teacher. He made house calls rather than have his home disrupted all day by students and their parents trooping through his . . . and his sisters' home as well . . . since they would have to use the common access stairwell. His wife Eleanor was rather intolerant of strangers, so it made sense to use the student's homes and pianos. She was an old fashion housewife who spent her days doing house chores and cooking . . . and taking afternoon naps.

When I met her, I assumed that she was much older than her husband, although in reality she was several years younger. I made a mental note hoping that my Helen would never age as fast as her sister-in-law obviously had.

Mike also played the organ at one of the neighboring towns Catholic churches, so he was up early mornings. Consequently, I saw little of him during our stay.

I found Tony and his wife, Eddis, quite agreeable. They had been most generous in sharing their time, their automobile and their home with us. Eddis was not Italian, but obviously had learned how to cook ethnic food from her in-laws. Her mother, who suffered from disabling arthritis, lived downstairs in their two-story home. While he didn't teach music, Tony was an accomplished pianist and violinist, and had played the latter instrument for a short time in the Hartford Symphony Orchestra. He also enjoyed writing an occasional piece of music for the piano.

His other major hobby was photography. He had his own dark room for developing pictures, and regaled us with slide shows of his original pictures several times during our stay. He took me aside while the women were in the kitchen and confided that he envied my becoming an officer.

"I was in the Army for a short time. I got sent to basic training in Florida and was all set to be a soldier when someone discovered that my right leg was shorter than my left."

He turned and showed me the built up heel on his right shoe.

"Had to make me even" he laughed.

"Just be glad that you're not a soldier when war comes" I answered rather sternly. Tony was briefly taken aback by my tone, but then realized there was no humor in combat where people die.

✧

The entire family gathered at the station to see us off. Tears were shed all around as we mounted the steps of our train car.

"You take good care yourself." Felix patted me on the shoulder as I mounted the steps of our car.

I was profoundly taken aback by these words coming from Helen's father. Somehow, there seemed to be an unspoken camaraderie between this soldier and the former militia man. Before I could respond, the steam whistle blew loudly and the wheels began to move, signaling the trains exit from the station. Everyone waved enthusiastically as tears fell from virtually everyone's eyes.

Somehow, the feeling seemed universal that we might never see one another again.

CHAPTER ELEVEN

We had only an hour before my bus left for Quantico once we arrived in Washington. We took a cab to Marine Corps Headquarters and then found a quiet corner in the coffee shop in the basement where we could be alone.

"I want you to know what a good time I had and how much I enjoyed meeting your family . . . I really mean that. Some men I know are uncomfortable when they visit their fiancée's home for the first time, but yours was truly special.

I especially liked your father. He projects a quiet intimacy.

And of course, every day is special when I'm with you."

Helen smiled coyly and held my hand tightly.

"Likewise for me. You know, my father is usually quiet and shy. But he connected with you . . . I think because you were both in the military."

She relaxed back into her chair.

"Now, when am I going to see you again?"

"Just as soon as I get checked into OCS and find out the schedule, I'll be in touch and arrange to get us together as soon as I can. You know that I'll be thinking about you the entire time that I'm away."

"You'd better try and keep your mind on what you're doing there. I want you to be number one in your class. Will there be any more combat training?"

"I'm not sure, but I don't think so. There will be daily physical workouts, of that I'm sure. They want us all to stay in shape . . . can't get too flabby if we're to set an example for the enlisted men and especially the new recruits."

"See" I said as I grabbed the skin just below my belt area.

Helen put her hand there and laughed.

"Why you haven't got an ounce of fat anywhere on that lean body of yours. I wish I could say the same."

I ogled her from top to bottom.

"The difference, my dear, is that you have lovely folds and bumps in all the right places."

"You're terrible."

"I know."

She blushed and then leaned into my waiting lips.

Just then a Marine corporal walked through the coffee shop announcing the impending departure of the Quantico bus.

"Well, I guess that's my cue to leave.

Walk me to the bus."

Helen was beginning to cry.

"No!

Just kiss me and go.

I don't want anyone to see me like this."

I gave her a final kiss and disappeared through the doorway assuring her that we'd be together soon.

I found the OCS schedule a bit more grueling than I had anticipated. Each day started with calisthenics followed by a one mile run. After a shower and breakfast, the remainder of the day was spent in classroom work. Then to conclude the day, the calisthenics and run were repeated.

I didn't mind the repetitive schedule so much as the fact that most weekends were allocated to taking duty call. There would be only two weekends available to see Helen in Washington. Not knowing what the future would hold upon completion of OCS and following my commissioning as a second lieutenant in the United States Marine Corps, I decided to make *our engagement official on the day of graduation. I had been saving what little money I could to buy an engagement ring for Helen. The Post Exchange carried a small selection of rings and I had spied one that I felt I could afford and that I thought Helen would approve of.*

At approximately the mid-point of the course, I had my first weekend off and took the Friday afternoon bus to Washington. Helen and I had corresponded almost daily by mail, but neither of us could wait for our next time together. She preferred that we spend the evening alone, so she arranged dinner at our favorite Italian restaurant, followed by seeing the premiere movie of the day, and then we returned to the hotel room that she had reserved for me.

"Isn't this getting a little risqué . . . I mean us alone in a hotel room together?"

"Oh Jim, I don't care what others may think. I love you and I know that you love me and that soon we can plan to be married.

Don't be a prude!"

With that encouragement, I grabbed her and pulled her close and kissed her as we tumbled onto the bed.

"Now, that's more like it soldier" she said while gazing into my eyes.

"Do you think we should go any further?"

Her answer was clear. She stood up and undressed exposing her breasts to me for the first time. I stood and caressed them, then helped her remove her remaining clothes as she removed mine.

"So, that's what making love is like."

"I hope I didn't hurt you."

"You could never hurt me, my darling.

You were wonderful."

"Well, you weren't so bad yourself. In fact, we were pretty good for first timers, don't you think?"

"You mean . . . this was your first time too?

I always thought Marines were known for taking advantage of women wherever they were, especially right after basic training."

"I always knew I would meet someone just like you and it would be perfect doing it for the first time together."

She snuggled up to me. By the next morning we had coupled several more times. She awoke with a big smile on her face.

I was already awake and studying her.

"What's the big grin for?"

"I just realized that I'm no longer a virgin!"

"Is that bad?"

"I don't think so.

But suppose we try it once more and then I'll let you know?"

The VCR suddenly stopped.

"Mother!"

Helen looked at Maria and just grinned.

"Did you think you were the product of an 'immaculate conception'? I'm sorry if it shocks you dear, but we were in love and war was at our doorstep. I loved your father so much and I didn't want him taken away from me without ever having professed our love in that way."

Maria expressed her understanding and said she only hoped she too could find a love like that. Then she pressed a button and the film flickered back to life on the screen.

We spent the weekend playing tourist . . . visiting the various monuments and walking along the reflection pool, but mostly in bed getting better acquainted. Lying next to me, with her nakedness completely exposed, Helen suddenly laughed.

"I wonder what my parents would think if they could see us now?"

I turned onto my side facing her.

"Did you ever think that maybe they did the same thing when they first met? That they were just like us and countless other young people in love who couldn't wait until they were married to experience the joy of sex?"

"Jim!"

She turned toward me and stared into my eyes.

"What an interesting thought. Somehow, I guess we never think of our parents having sex . . . before or after marriage. But then, if they didn't where would we be? Although my parents came from Italy, they didn't meet until

they were in New York . . . but then I guess that doesn't change anything. We wouldn't ever hear about it if they did have sex before marriage . . . it's just not something people talk about."

I cupped her right breast dangling free in front of me.

"You are making a loose woman out of me, Jim Mathews."

"I seem to remember it was you that started all this by undressing in front of me."

She responded by kissing me firmly on the mouth and then rolling onto her back for one last love making session before I had to dress for my trip back to Quantico.

"I don't know if I'll be able to get back before graduation. If not, I'll expect to see you there on December 5th. I hope some of your family will be able to come as well."

"I doubt that . . . they never travel any distance from home. Since they moved to Connecticut from New York, I think the farthest away they've been is to the beach at Hammonasset . . . and then only to sit and watch the waves. I've never seen my parents in bathing suits."

"I'll write you about arrangements for your stay and for the weekend to follow. We'll have to plan something really big."

She accompanied me to the bus station and kissed me a final time.

"Well, Lieutenant, I'll see you soon."

"Not lieutenant quite yet, but soon . . . Mrs. Mathews."

As the bus departed, I could see the huge grin on her face and I smiled.

Chapter Twelve

Unfortunately, there were no more breaks in the OCS schedule, so we had to be content with letters . . . usually daily . . . and an infrequent phone call. We mutually decided that while we loved to hear each other's voice, the expense was just too much.

Graduation was fast approaching and we were eager to see me get my lieutenant's bars. While post-graduation assignments weren't official yet, I had it on good authority that I would most likely be assigned to the Navy Department in Washington, D.C. where the Marines had a fairly large presence, both in security details and various liaison billets. The original plan to send me to the officer's basic school after graduation had been shelved for the time being due to the world situation. The Corps felt it more important to get me to my assignment right away so that I would be prepared to help the war effort immediately if and when it came.

Helen was busy planning for the trip to Quantico the day before graduation and I was busy making arrangements for her stay at the best hotel in town. In addition, I had purchased the engagement ring that I had been eyeing at the Post Exchange with plans to ask Helen the big important question that night after graduation.

Thursday, December 4, 1941 arrived a cold, blustery day in Quantico, Virginia. Fortunately, there had been no precipitation and the prediction for the following day was for a brief warm up with temperatures expected to reach almost sixty degrees. The graduation ceremonies were scheduled to take place in doors, but the thought of a warm and sunny early winter day was pleasing to Helen, me and all my fellow Marine graduates to be.

Her bus arrived only a few minutes past the five p.m. scheduled arrival time. I was there anxiously waiting.

"Hey there, you" I said as she slid into my waiting embrace.

"You feel good".

"Do you have a checked bag?"

She handed me the claim ticket and stood curbside as I accompanied the driver to the baggage compartment on the side of the bus.

"Thank you, sir" the driver said as I handed him a tip.

"My, you must have brought everything you own" I said referring to the weight of the suitcase.

"A girl has to be dressed properly for occasions such as this. It's not every day that her man becomes an officer in the Marine Corps."

"Now, let's get you to your hotel room. I'm sure we have some catching up to do."

I winked and she blushed, remembering our last time together.

As soon as we were settled in the hotel room, it took only a few moments for us to undress for the first of many times during our weekend together.

"You must be starved" I said, as we lay facing each other.

"I was, but that can wait. Somehow I don't feel hungry when I'm here with you. Perhaps we can go out a little later?"

I took that as my cue to make love to her again. She was eager to please me as well as to satisfy her own needs.

"Now" she said after the second round of intimacy, "I am famished."

"Well, you should be. I think we both just worked off a few pounds."

I just layed there and smiled and listened to her chuckled response.

The morning of December 5, 1941 arrived and as predicted was clear and sunny. The morning temperature had dipped to thirty-nine degrees, but by nine a.m. it was already reaching well into the forties en route to a predicted high of sixty-two degrees.

I had arisen at six a.m. and left for my quarters to dress for the ceremony. I would be wearing full dress blues and for the first time in my career as a Marine, an officer's cap. The gold band that sat above the visor would be presented to us at the ceremony.

Since none of Helen's family or my mother had been able to make the trip to Quantico, I had arranged for one of my classmate's family to escort her to the festivities. We would meet at the conclusion of the ceremony . . . right after the official swearing in of the new officers and the presentation of our new rank and cap insignia.

The ceremonies began with the class marching in and taking their places at the front of the auditorium. This was followed by a procession of dignitaries. When all were in place, the base Marine band struck up "The Star Spangled Banner" followed by a rousing rendition of the "Marine Corps Hymn".

The official ceremony was presided over by the commandant of the OCS school, Colonel John McNulty, who in turn introduced the Assistant to the Commandant of the Marine Corps, Brigadier General Charles D. Barrett, who would give the major commencement address.

> *"My fellow Marines, today you join the ranks of the officers*
> *of the finest fighting force the world has ever known. As the*
> *Hymn refrains 'From the halls of Montezuma to the shores*
> *of Tripoli' . . . from the date of our founding on November 10,*
> *1775, the Corps has been proud to serve our nation in any*
> *capacity requested of us.*
> *You will be asked to serve in that same capacity, and I have*
> *no doubt that you will respond as all those who have served*
> *before you have . . . with courage, honor and conviction.*
> *The world stands at a dangerous crossroads as we speak and*
> *it is virtually inevitable that each of you will be called upon to*
> *serve your country in some war time capacity in the near future.*
> *So, it is my honor to represent the commandant of the Marine*

Corps in welcoming you to the ranks of the officer corps. And to
each of you a hearty 'Semper Fi'."

With the conclusion of the general's remarks, the entire class stood.
Colonel McNulty then assembled the officials into a line for presentation
of our diplomas, our promotion papers to second lieutenant, our new collar
rank insignia and gold cap bands denoting the officer rank. Additionally,
each of us was given a set of orders with our new duty assignment and report
date.

At the completion of the ceremony, everyone rose to sing a chorus of the
"Marine Corps Hymn" followed by "America the Beautiful".

We all cheered and flung our caps into the air and then filed out as we
had entered to await the well wishes from friends and family.

∽

"Come here you handsome devil and let me kiss you."

I must admit I felt resplendent in my dress blues now regaled with
officer's bars and an officer's hat with gold braid.

"Well, did you get the assignment you were expecting?"

I glanced at the envelope containing my orders that I was holding in my
hand.

"I haven't had a chance to look."

I opened the envelope and read the orders aloud to Helen.

"You are hereby granted ten (10) days authorized leave of absence,
following which you are ordered to report to NavDept, WashDC for duty, no
later than 1700hrs, 15 December 1941.

Report to commander, MarCorp planning division for further
instructions.

You are authorized, et cetera, et cetera . . . .

The rest is just logistics having to do with pay and allowances."

"So what exactly does that mean you'll be doing?"

"I think it's the war planning section for the Marines Corps. It's located
in the Navy Department since the corps is technically a part of the Navy. The
good news, my darling, is that we'll be together in Washington for at least a
year or two.

Now, I have about three hours worth of things I need to do before I can
be clear of this place. So let's get something to eat at the reception and then

I'll have the folks that brought you here escort you back to the hotel where I will meet you just as soon as I can.

And then I have a little surprise for you this evening."

Helen knew what she wanted the surprise to be but felt it best to let me do it my own way.

"I can't wait."

CHAPTER THIRTEEN

I arrived at Helen's hotel room about an hour later than I had planned. Upon returning to my room, I was confronted by several of my classmates who felt we should celebrate the occasion with a beer or two at the Officer's Club that we were now entitled to use. I tried to resist, but they played upon my emotions, suggesting that it might be the last time we would be together for a long time . . . if ever should war come. I indicated to them that I would have to keep it short since I had very important plans for the evening. Knowing that Helen was in town, they chided me about what exactly those plans might entail. I took the kidding in stride but refused to divulge exactly what those plans were.

They were strictly private between me and Helen.

"Sorry I'm late, but the guys wouldn't let me get away."
She put her arms around my neck and pulled me close.
"That's all right . . . you're here now and that's all that counts. I'm just so proud of you. Now, kiss me."
I held her tightly and we kissed deep and long.

"Now, just what was the big surprise you mentioned?"

I took a step back towards the door where I had hung my coat and hat. I reached into my coat pocket and brought out a small box. As I turned back toward Helen, I took a step and then bent down on one knee. I opened the small box containing the ring and held it up toward her.

"Helen Brand, you are the love of my life. Since the day that I met you I have dreamed of this moment.

Will you do me the honor of marrying me?"

She wanted to act surprised but couldn't hold back the fact that it was what she had anticipated ever since I had hinted at it some months ago when the rumor of my appointment to OCS had first surfaced.

"Oh yes, yes, yes.

A thousand times yes!"

I stood up and placed the ring on her left fourth finger.

"It's beautiful" was all she could say.

She looked up at me motioning for me to kiss her.

I gladly obliged.

"I love you" I whispered.

"I love you too."

"Now, I took the liberty to make reservations for dinner at the Officer's Club. I hear they have the best steak and seafood in town. And it will give me a chance to show you off to my fellow officers."

"If you think I'm pretty enough?"

"You'll be the prettiest girl there and the only one that my eyes will be on all evening."

She took another longing look at the new ring on her finger.

"I can't wait to tell my friends and family."

I had arranged a table for two set with candles in the rear of the club where we could be alone on this most special of evenings. As we entered the club, I stopped to introduce Helen to several of my classmates and the commandant and his wife.

"Colonel McNulty, may I present my fiancée, Helen Brand."

Helen turned to face the colonel and his wife.

"Jim, I didn't know you were hiding such a lovely lady . . . fiancée you say?"

"We just got engaged this evening, sir."

Colonel McNulty turned to his wife and made the introductions. She took one look at Helen and reached for her hand.

"My how lovely" she said, eyeing Helen's engagement ring.

After a few pleasantries, the Colonel and his wife excused themselves.

"We're sure that you two would like to be alone on this special occasion" Mrs. McNulty offered.

"Please enjoy the evening."

We took our seats at the waiting table. A few minutes later, the waiter came and presented us a magnum of champagne.

"Compliments of Colonel and Mrs. McNulty" he said, gesturing toward the commandant's table.

"Please thank them for us" I responded. The waiter placed two glasses on the table and filled each to the brim with champagne.

"To us."

"To us" she repeated.

"Now and forever".

ℐ

We spent a cozy evening together back at Helen's room. Awaking early the next morning, I rolled over and placed my hand on Helen's hip.

"Good morning, Mrs. Mathews to be".

She opened her eyes and looked at me and smiled. She took my hand and placed it on her breast.

"How about a little bit of that early morning loving that you're so good at?"

I certainly didn't hesitate a bit. When we were done, I rolled back over and gently went to sleep. The next thing I remembered was Helen coming out of the bathroom with a towel wrapped around her head.

"I thought you were going to sleep all day."

"What time is it?"

"It's almost eleven. If we're going to get to Washington today, we'd better get a move on. The next bus leaves at one and check out time here is noon."

I motioned to Helen to sit at the bedside.

"Now don't go getting any more romantic ideas. We've really got to get going."

"Don't think that thought hadn't entered my mind. But, you're right."

I kissed her once more, then got out of bed and headed straight for the bathroom.

⁊

We arrived in Washington at about five p.m. and took a cab to Helen's boarding house. As soon as she was settled, I said I needed to find a place to stay and thought I would be able to be quartered at Marine Corps headquarters which was nearby. Helen said she was sure that one of the male occupants of the boarding house was gone for the weekend and had left his key with the landlady for me. When she checked, indeed he had.

"Now, that's settled.

You'll be right down the hall from me . . . that is, unless you can think of a reason to sneak back here during the night."

"You're terrible" was all I could say.

"But, that's why I love you. I'd hate to think what it would be like to be around someone with no sense of adventure."

After I was settled in my room, we decided to go to Georgetown for dinner and a movie.

"Do you like Humphrey Bogart? I think he's so neat the way he talks" Helen asked me.

"Well, I don't really know . . . exactly who is he?"

"Silly.

He's a very popular movie star and he's in 'All Through the Night' and it's playing at the Loew's theatre right near where I planned for us to eat dinner. So it's settled . . . dinner and then Humphrey Bogart."

I kissed her once again and threw up his hands.

"Whatever you say, dear" . . . a phrase that I would repeat many times over during the coming years.

⁊

After the movie, we decided that we both needed some rest after the events of the past week. After seeing Helen to her room at the boarding house, I headed directly to mine. I was asleep immediately and stayed that way for the next eight hours as did Helen.

The following morning after a late breakfast, we elected to spend a leisurely day sightseeing. There were many sights that I had not seen and

Helen looked forward to chauffeuring me around. The weather was predicted to be moderately warm and clear for early December, so we planned to take full advantage of it while we could. Winters could be notoriously cold in Washington.

After a stroll through several of the buildings of the Smithsonian, we climbed the five hundred and fifty-five steps of the Washington monument again.

"What a wonderful view from up here" I commented. "Even though I've been here before, the view is always breathtaking."

"Jim, I don't think I'm up to walking all the way down after climbing up" Helen retorted.

"I'm going to have to put you on a physical exercise regimen if you're going to be married to a Marine. Just this once we'll take the elevator."

She glanced my way, not sure if I was serious or not. As we exited the monument, crowds of people were stirring around in an unusually hurried manner. Perplexed by the anxious looks on the faces of numerous passersby, I spied a Marine in uniform and asked what was going on?"

"Haven't you heard, Sir? It's just been announced on the radio that the Japs have attacked Pearl Harbor in the Hawaiian Islands.

It looks like we're going to war!"

Chapter Fourteen

"Jim, what's going to happen to us and our plans?"

Helen's eyes were full of tears as the news of the attack on Pearl Harbor began to sink in. Everyone around us had a fearful look as details trickled in. A few cheered, noting that America's entrance into the war had been inevitable and that we were late taking our place.

I held Helen close as we continued walking along the mall.

"Now, don't you go jumping the gun. I need to report to my duty station and get the facts. As soon as I have more exact information, I'll be able to tell you what may happen and when.

In the mean time, consider our plans as good as gold."

I did my best to reassure Helen that things would be all right, although deep inside I knew that being transferred to a unit preparing for war was assuredly going to take me into it. Convincing myself that things would be all right was all but impossible.

"Let me take you back to the boarding house and then I'm going to the Navy Department to see what I can find out."

"You promise you won't leave me?"

I mumbled a response knowing that I couldn't in good faith make such a promise that I would almost certainly have to break.

"I'm Lieutenant Mathews . . . ."

The Navy Chief at the reception desk inside the main entrance to the Navy Department abruptly interrupted me.

"Sir, we have been instructed by SecNav to have all officers and enlisted men report to their units immediately. All leaves are cancelled until further notice. Further information about the status of the military in Hawaii and other strategic locations will be forthcoming and reported through your unit. President Roosevelt also plans a national address sometime within the next twenty-four hours. It will be carried on all radio stations locally and nationally."

"Thank you, Chief. One more thing, can you direct me to the 'Planning Division'?"

"Let me get someone to take you there. It's a little difficult to find."

A young Navy seaman appeared and motioned me to follow him to the section inside the Navy Department headquarters building.

"This way, Sir."

The Chief was quite right. Getting to the Planning Division involved numerous twists and turns along parallel passageways in the rather lengthy building situated along Constitution Avenue. When we finally arrived at a section clearly marked as Marine Corps space, we had to pass through several large work areas before we finally arrived at the "Planning Division".

"Here you are, Sir."

"Thank you, Seaman."

I surveyed the small space that apparently would be my new home. I noted a sergeant toward the rear of the room. As I entered, the sergeant turned toward me.

"Good afternoon, Lieutenant, may I help you?"

"I'm Lieutenant James Mathews. I was due to report for duty in about eight days . . . but it looks like my plans have been changed rather abruptly."

"I'm Sergeant Brooks, sir. We were expecting you in about a week, but I guess things have changed dramatically. I'm sorry to meet you under such circumstances, sir, but welcome to our small home.

Colonel Lowry, our CO, is TDY in Virginia, but he'll be back by tonight. He just contacted me about an hour ago, right after the news of the attack was announced. He has asked that everyone report here at 0730 tomorrow morning.

Do you have a place to stay, sir?"

"Yes, thank you.

If you're sure there's nothing I can do now, I'll plan to see you and the colonel tomorrow."

"Very good, sir. Until tomorrow."

✍

"Didn't they give you any idea what you might have to do if war is declared?" An element of terror was obvious in Helen's voice. And just when she was beginning to feel that her life was coming together . . . just when she had found the man of her dreams who had declared his love and commitment to her . . . this had to happen. Yes, it had been a possibility . . . perhaps even more realistically a probability . . . for some time.

But why now and why this dramatic?

She looked at the shiny ring on her finger . . . a symbol of my love that had been placed there a mere forty-eight hours earlier. She should be planning our wedding, not having to worry if I would be whisked off to war with the possibility that I may never return.

She put her head against my chest and began to cry. I knew there was nothing I could say that would console her, so I just held her tight and let her weep.

✍

"Mr. Vice-President, Mr. Speaker, members of the Senate and House of Representatives:

Yesterday, December 7, 1941—a date which will live in infamy—the United States of America was suddenly and deliberately attacked by naval and air forces of the Empire of Japan.

The United States was at peace with that nation, and, at the solicitation of Japan, was still in conversation with its government and its Emperor looking toward the maintenance of peace in the Pacific . . . .

As Commander-in-Chief of the Army and Navy I have directed that all measures be taken for our defense, that always will our whole nation remember the character of the onslaught against us.

No matter how long it may take us to overcome this premeditated invasion, the American people, in their righteous might, will win through to absolute victory . . . .

I ask that the Congress declare that since the unprovoked and dastardly attack by Japan on Sunday, December 7, 1941, a state of war has existed between the United States and the Japanese Empire."

❦

I along with Colonel Lowry and the other members of the Planning Division listened, as had virtually the entire nation, to President Roosevelt addressing a joint session of Congress carried on virtually every radio station from coast to coast.

After the conclusion, the colonel turned to the group.

"Well, there you have it. It's official. We're at war with Japan, and unless I'm mistaken, we'll soon be at war with the rest of her allies as well. Germany and Italy have just been itching to get us into their conflict in Europe. England could certainly use our help. I'm frankly surprised that we didn't get into the European conflict a long time ago considering our friendship with Churchill and Great Britain.

I expect that our orders will be forthcoming from the War Department within the next twenty-four to forty-eight hours. So, gentlemen, I would suggest that you spend what little remaining time you might have with your families and loved ones. We very well may be deployed closer to the Pacific campaign headquarters which will either be on the West coast or possibly even in the Hawaiian Islands, depending on whether or not Japan invades them in their time of helplessness.

Please check back here at 0700 tomorrow morning. I'm sure we'll have heard something of interest by then even if we don't have official moving orders."

We all looked at one another.

"Yes Sir" we all replied in unison.

❦

It took me approximately thirty-five minutes to reach Helen at the boarding house. Most everyone had stayed home to hear the President's address.

"You've got bad news, don't you?" It was difficult to hide anything from her.

"As you probably heard, President Roosevelt has just addressed Congress and war has been officially declared against Japan. I need to report back

early in the morning and find out exactly what my outfit has been ordered to do. It could possibly involve relocation to the West coast or Hawaii."

Already I could see the tears forming in the corners of her eyes. I squeezed her hand and pulled her close to me.

"Of course, it may take weeks or more for our mobilization orders to be cut and things readied to move a whole section . . . if it comes to that. In the mean time, let's just enjoy each other's company as usual."

Once again, she quietly placed her head on my chest and silently wept.

CHAPTER FIFTEEN

Colonel Lowry was totally forthcoming as soon as the entire group had assembled.

"SecNav has ordered our entire unit to proceed to the west coast to the new training area, Camp Pendleton, as soon as possible. We'll be quartered there at least for the time being. It's entirely possible that we could be ordered from there to Camp Smith on Oahu if the Japs don't invade the island.

Preliminary indications are that there have been no further attacks on the island or any others in the Hawaiian chain. What aircraft that were spared have been flying lookout up to fifty miles out in a three hundred and sixty degree circumference around the islands, and so far there has been no sign of the Japanese fleet. No one has been able to explain exactly why they appear to have hightailed it home after devastating our fleet at Pearl. It would seem that they could have taken over the entire island if they had bombed our oil reserves and other air strips . . . but that's not the case, thank God.

Jim, I'm going to ask you to take Sgt. Schmidt and Corporal Lewis and board a train for California first thing in the morning. You'll be our advance team and will be responsible for getting things set up so that we can get right to work when the entire unit arrives. I would anticipate that the rest of us should be there within thirty to forty-five days."

The colonel could see my reaction and knew the hardship it was going to place on my personal life.

"Lieutenant, please take your two men and proceed to transportation where your orders and tickets will be waiting. Then, take the rest of the day off. I'm sure you all have things to settle with your families. And Jim, notify me as soon as you arrive at Pendleton.

Good luck, men."

The men turned and proceeded as ordered. My heart was heavy as I contemplated having to tell Helen that this would be our last night together for the foreseeable future . . . if not forever.

"Oh, Jim. It's what I've feared most since the day I met you. I remember the first time I came to Parris Island and you had to leave suddenly. At least then we weren't at war. Does anyone have any idea how long this war could last?"

There was no good answer to such a question as that.

"Darling, hopefully as soon as our forces can get geared up, it will take just a short while to force the Japanese back to where they belong . . . on their own small group of islands far, far away from the U.S. It's amazing that they were able to carry out such a bold attack so far away from their homeland. But we have a new technology that hopefully will prevent such surprises in the future."

Helen indicated that she didn't understand what I was referring to.

"It's called radar . . . it stands for _radio detecting and ranging_."

She looked even more puzzled.

"What that means is a radio beam is sent out and when it strikes something solid it sends back an image. The time it takes for the beam to return to its source helps determine the distance away from the source. The British are already using it against the Germans."

Helen smiled and squeezed my hand.

"Well, why didn't you just say that the first time?"

It was evident to me that she still had no real comprehension of what I had just said.

"Take my word for it, it will be an important tool in this war . . . and hopefully will help keep it short so that I can come home to you soon. And when I do, the first thing I'll want to do is marry you and start that family we've talked about."

She grabbed me around the neck, pulled me close and kissed me full on the lips.

"Perhaps you can show me just how that's done tonight?"

I grabbed her around the waist and together we headed for the bedroom.

I asked her not to come to Union Station for my send off.

"It would be too emotional for both of us".

But, there she was, standing at a distance as my men and I gathered our things together for the long journey west.

"Lieutenant, isn't that your fiancée standing over there?"

"Yes, Sergeant, it is. I had preferred she not come but she insisted. I hate to see women cry . . . not to mention men."

The porter announced that the train would be leaving in five minutes.

"I'm going to say one last goodbye. Please see to my things and I'll join you in our car shortly."

"You know this just makes things harder."

"I know" Helen answered.

"But I couldn't stand it after you left the apartment. I just had to come down here and see you off."

"If I knew I had only one more day to live, last night would have been just the way I would have wanted to spend it . . . with you."

"Oh Jim. I love you so much. Take good care of yourself and come back to me. Call me as soon as you can."

Helen was crying and I did all I could to hold back the tears I could feel forming in the corners of my eyes.

"All aboard!"

We both turned toward the train as it prepared to depart. I gave her one more quick kiss and then ran to join my men.

The trek across country took almost three days with all the stops and train changes necessary. After arriving in Los Angeles, we took a bus to the small town of Oceanside.

"Just where the hell are we Lieutenant?" asked Schmidt.

"Sergeant, this wide open space here will soon be transformed into the largest Marine Corps base in the country. According to something I read it was once one of the largest cattle ranches in the country. It was started in 1863.

They've begun construction on quarters for those of us reporting in urgently. We just have to find out exactly where they are."

Signage on the fledgling base was poor to non-existent, but we finally located the small headquarters building. From there, we were directed to our temporary quarters.

"I would've expected something like this in a battle zone, but not here!"

"Corporal Lewis, you wouldn't be pleased if the Ritz was here" Sergeant Schmidt added.

"Gentlemen, I'm an officer and I'm not supposed to complain in front of my troops . . . so I won't . . . but I agree with Lewis."

Our quarters consisted of small wooden shacks each with a single door and window. The interior was equally spartan with bunks, each with a rolled mattress on top. There was a small wood stove for heating. While the weather along the California coastline was generally temperate, there were periods of cool temperatures and extreme dampness frequently associated with dense fog. An adjacent building held bathing and toilet facilities.

"Well, men, let's get situated here. Then we need to get some chow before we report back to headquarters and get working."

It didn't take long to stow our gear. The mess hall was adjacent to the headquarters building, so we hurried back and sat down to a warm meal before getting down to business. At headquarters, the G-3 was trying to get things organized for the onslaught of arriving troops and supplies.

"Lieutenant Mathews, I'm Major Pickens. I want you to be my plans and training officer . . . a dual job for the time being. I understand from your records that you've spent time at Parris Island as a DI."

"Yes, sir. I just finished OCS training, and had barely reported to headquarters in Washington when the Japanese decided to drag us into this war. But, most of us knew it was coming and were expecting it at any time. However, sir, it caught me at a particularly bad time."

"How's that, Lieutenant?"

"Well, sir, I just got engaged the night of graduation from OCS, and was thrilled that I was assigned to duty in Washington. That's where my fiancée lives and works. As you might imagine, she . . . and I . . . weren't too happy about the news on the seventh."

"Nor were any of us. But, we have our jobs to perform, so what do you say we all get to work? Now, first of all, my name is Walter, but most people just call me 'Walt'. And how about you, Lieutenant?"

"James, but everyone calls me 'Jim'. The sergeant usually goes by 'Smitty', and Lewis . . . well, we just call him 'Slick'."

"Where'd you ever get that moniker, corporal?"

"Well, Sir, I'm kind of handy with the ladies, if you catch my drift. So the guys labeled me 'Slick'."

Everyone shared a laugh.

"There's certainly nothing wrong with a talent like that, son, but I'm afraid you won't have much time to put it to use out here for the foreseeable future."

"Yes, sir."

"Now, Jim I want you to take your men and survey the base property. I've got a map here that shows what facilities are already here and several that are proposed but not built yet. We're going to be getting a lot of troops in soon who'll form the First Marine Division. They're a remnant of the I Marine Expeditionary Force from WWI.

We're going to need quarters, dining facilities and training grounds. As soon as their advance contingency arrives in about two weeks, I'm going to put you to work along with their plans people on mapping out our part in the war. I'm told we could be deploying a division in as little as three or four months from now."

"I'm you man, Walt. Just point me in the right direction."

Nineteen forty-two came fast and things at Camp Pendleton were at full fury. I and my men surveyed the land and made proposals to the command for implementation of construction of the various components of a major training center.

In February, hierarchy of the 5th regiment, a component of the 1st Marine Division, reported to the base thereby relieving me and my men of primary responsibility for the facilities development for the time being. Troops followed and after only two months training, they disembarked and were deployed to Wellington, New Zealand where they would await the arrival of elements of the 7th regiment and several battalions of the 5th that were currently scattered across the Pacific. Numerous problems including a dock workers strike kept them in New Zealand until late July, nineteen forty-two.

Eventually, they would be transported to the Solomon Islands where they came under control of naval forces commanded by Vice-Admiral Frank Fletcher. After a month of landing rehearsals, they embarked on the real thing, landing on the island of Guadalcanal in the Solomon group on August 7.

"My dearest Helen,

It's so nice that you can find time to write me almost every day. I don't know what I would do if I couldn't look forward to your letters. I'm only sorry that I can't call you more often . . . I love hearing your voice. You're always so positive about things. If I had more time, I'd write every day too, but things here are buzzing like bees in a hive.

I can't go into any detail . . . security you understand . . . but the 1st Marine Division is getting ready to move and we'll undoubtedly get more troops in here as soon as they're gone. It's hard to complain about the weather here. Most days are clear after some early morning fog and the temperatures are quite moderate . . . nothing like back in D.C. or even the Carolinas. If I knew that I would be here for an extended period of time, I would ask you to join me. But things are constantly changing as news from the Pacific comes in.

I hope that your job doesn't keep you so busy that you don't have time to think of me often. Know that I think of you during every waking moment of my day.

Love always,

Jim

CHAPTER SIXTEEN

The war was still in its infancy in the spring of nineteen forty-two. The devastating attack at Pearl Harbor had left the United States Navy in shambles. The better part of its fleet of destroyers, battleships and carriers had either been destroyed or rendered unusable for a significant period of time. The ship repair facilities had been equally laid low by the Japanese torpedoes.

The mood of the military and the American public was somber as they were forced to sit and listen to the reports of additional Japanese victories and conquests across the Pacific. Unknown to most, a plan had been devised in early January, nineteen forty-two to retaliate for the Pearl Harbor attack. Imperialistic Japan had convinced itself and its people that they and their military were invincible.

Navy Captain Francis Low presented his plan to Admiral Ernest King on January 10 of that year after observing the B-25s taking off from a shortened runway marked with the dimensions of a carrier deck. President Roosevelt endorsed the daring plan and Colonel James (Jimmy) Doolittle was selected to lead the sixteen craft squadron on a bombing raid directly over Tokyo. Their payloads would do minimal damage at best, but the psychological effect on the Japanese people and the Japanese hierarchy would be immense.

After the craft chosen to participate in the raid were modified and lightened at Minneapolis, they were flown to Eglin Field in Florida where their crews spent three grueling weeks learning to take off on a simulated short deck mimicking the carrier USS Hornet. Then the craft were flown to California and loaded onto the Hornet at Alameda. On April 2, they set sail for a rendezvous with the USS Enterprise under the command of Vice Admiral William F. Halsey, awaiting them just north of the Hawaiian Islands.

The task force set sail for Japan; the intent was to launch the raid from a point about four hundred miles east of Japan. However, on the morning of April 18, a Japanese picket boat sighted the fleet and quickly radioed Japan of their presence. The fleet was approximately six hundred and fifty miles from the shores of Honshu. From that distance, the fuel onboard each plane would be inadequate to return to the carriers after delivering their ordnance over Tokyo. A decision was quickly made to launch from that point, knowing that the planes would have to ditch somewhere over the Chinese mainland after the raid. The plan was presented to the "Raiders" and they all agreed to participate. Within forty minutes of their discovery by the Japanese craft, all sixteen B-25s were safely off the deck of Hornet en route to Tokyo. Within six hours, the raiders had dropped their bombs over Tokyo, Yokohama and several nearby cities. Fifteen of the aircraft proceeded to crash landings in China and one in Russia.

Eventually, all but three of the raiders returned home. What Colonel Doolittle initially thought was a failed raid came to be known as one of the most daring exploits of the war and was a major morale booster to the military and the American public in general.

"It's so good to hear your voice, my darling."

I saved up enough to make a transcontinental call, something that was quite expensive in the era of WWII, as it was now being called. I had to drive into the nearby community of Oceanside to find a telephone booth and then endure the ten minutes worth of call transfers before finally hearing the phone ring in Helen's boarding house.

Then several agonizing and expensive minutes passed before she reached the phone.

"How are things in California?

Are you safe and warm there?

Any news on whether or not you'll be transferred?"

"Whoa . . . not so many questions.

Things are fine, and yes . . . I'm safe and warm.

As to the transfer, I think I'll be safe here for a while yet, but given my background as a drill instructor, I think they'll probably want me to lead a squadron into battle at some point. I'm not sure what division I may be assigned to just yet. They're talking about activating several more divisions and they should be passing through here over the next six to twelve months.

So, don't you worry that pretty face of yours one bit.

Now, tell me how you've been and what's new in Washington?"

We talked for what seemed only a minute when the operator injected herself into the conversation and asked that I deposit an additional five dollars.

"Oh, Jim, you can't afford that."

"Don't you worry. I came prepared with fifteen dollars worth of quarters."

I deposited the coins.

"Now, talk away."

The conversation drifted from one topic to another, with both of us trying to stave off the time when we would have to hang up.

"Helen, I want you to come out here. I've checked and I can get you an apartment just off the base."

"Jim, I don't know . . . I mean you could be transferred at any time. How about if I come for a week or ten days? Will you have any leave time coming at all?"

"I'll have to check with my C.O . . . . that's my commanding officer."

"I'm sure I can arrange something if you can."

The operator once again broke in to announce that I had one minute left on my fifteen minute call.

"Well, I guess I'll have to hang up now; I've used up all my quarters. I'll let you know about taking leave as soon as I can. I can't wait to see you again and hold you."

"Me too, Jim."

The line suddenly went dead as I realized that another minute had passed without additional money being deposited.

I didn't even get to add "I love you" before the connection was broken.

"Damn phones!"

ॐ

The next major victory and the first actual defeat for Japan began early on the morning of May 7, 1942 when Japanese and American carrier forces engaged each other in the Battle of the Coral Sea off the coast of New Guinea. It was the first time in history that a major battle occurred without the ships actually sighting one another. As had been predicted several decades earlier by Colonel Billy Mitchell and others, aircraft would be the new weapon of choice in war.

This was followed fairly quickly by a major defeat of the Japanese fleet at the Battle of Midway. The Americans had succeeded in breaking the Japanese code and knew that Japan intended to invade Midway Island in the hopes of securing a land based airfield for their fighters. Carrier scout planes located the Japanese task force heading northwest of Midway Island. The American fleet under command of Admiral Jack Fletcher aboard Yorktown, ordered Admiral Ray Spruance, in command of carriers Enterprise and Hornet to launch the attack as soon as the information was received. The decision to deploy their planes and intercept the Japanese fleet resulted in the loss of four carriers thanks to a series of errors on the part of the Japanese command and the perseverance of the American pilots. Yorktown, which had been damaged at Coral Sea and hurriedly repaired at Pearl Harbor allowing her to participate in the battle, was lost.

ॐ

In early August of the same year, the 1ˢᵗ Marine Division which had trained at Pendleton and deployed to Australia, invaded the island of Guadalcanal in the Solomon Islands. The battle for control of that island and several neighboring islands raged on until the last day of the year, severely testing the mettle of troops on both sides. But the final victory came to the Americans and the critically important airfield on the main island, now renamed Henderson Field, transferred securely into the hands of the Allied troops.

ॐ

The war effort consumed all of my time and there had not been an opportunity to take leave. However, as the year nineteen forty-two was nearing an end, I received notice that I would be assigned to duty with the newly forming 4th Marine Division, and that I would be granted ten days leave before reporting back to Pendleton for duty with my new group. As soon as I had official orders with the specific dates for the final days at my current assignment and my report date for my new assignment, I was on the phone with Helen. My ten days off would coincide with the Christmas and New Year's holidays.

"Helen, I've checked the train schedules. You can leave Union Station at five p.m. on December nineteenth and arrive in Los Angeles around noon on the twenty-second. You only have to change trains once in Chicago."

"I already mentioned going to California with my boss and he said any time I need to take off to see you will be fine. So I'll make the arrangements and let you know when I'll be leaving and what time I'll arrive.

Will you be able to meet me in Los Angeles?"

"One of my fellow officers here has a car that he's going to let me borrow. I figure we can spend a day or two in Los Angeles and then I'll bring you down here and show you off."

"Oh, Jim. That's the sweetest thing you've said about me in a long time."

"I'll be counting the days until you get here. Call me back as soon as you can.

I love you, my darling."

"And I love you too."

I stood staring forlornly into space as the dial tone hummed in my ear.

The eighteenth arrived and I spent my last day with the outfit I had been with for over a year now. I had come to appreciate the efforts that the behind the scenes sections made in the war effort. Fighting was the essence of war, but planning and logistics were what made it all possible. It would make little sense to have men transported to some remote island in the Pacific, and then not have provisions for food and ammunition to reach them; or to not have air cover when necessary or transport ships if they needed to be evacuated.

The thought of going into battle was a bit daunting as well, but I had trained hard in my early days in the Corps, and had spent a good deal of time training others in the art of combat. So I was prepared both mentally and physically for whatever might come my way. But for now, my thoughts were with Helen and her arrival in Los Angeles four days hence.

What I was not prepared for was the news that arrived the following morning. A Western Union messenger delivered the telegram just as I was preparing to depart Camp Pendleton for Los Angeles where I was going to find a hotel for my rendezvous with Helen.

The message was brief.

> *"Dad died unexpectedly this morning.*
> *Proceeding home to Connecticut for funeral.*
> *Details later.*
> *Sorry I will not be able to make it to California.*
> *Miss you.*
>
> *Love, Helen."*

I was stunned. I thought about taking a flight to be with her, but I knew I couldn't afford that. A train trip would take up all of my leave time. So, I settled on sitting tight until I heard from her again. This was a turn of events that was untimely and wholly undeserved for all concerned. I didn't want to seem selfish, but I missed Helen so much and knew she felt the same. But some things are utterly beyond human control.

A second telegram arrived early the following day. Helen was home and arrangements were being made for her father's funeral. She was sorry for the unfortunate turn of events, but family obligations superseded all others.

I stood and read and reread her words, especially the closing remarks:

> *"I miss you and will always love you.*
> *Take care my darling and let me hear from you soon.*
> *Yours, Helen."*

Once again, I headed into town to the nearest phone booth, armed with a pocketful of quarters. I wasn't sure when, if at all, there was a good time to call given the circumstances. I only hoped that she was at home and not out making arrangements for the funeral.

"Hello."

It was Helen's voice.

"Helen, I'm so sorry to hear about your father. He was an amazing man. You know how much I cared for him even though we only shared a short time together.

How are you and the family holding up?"

"Oh Jim.

I wish you could be here. Everyone is doing all right, but it's really hard to lose someone that you've loved and lived with your whole life. Mom is devastated. She and Dad were married for over fifty years.

Can you imagine what it will be like when we've been married that long?"

"Fifty years is certainly a long time.

Helen, I wish there was a way that I could be there with you, but you understand how long it would take for me to get there even if I could afford to fly."

"I understand. I know that you will be here in spirit with me, and I'll be thinking about you the whole time. I wish I could have made the trip to California, but I know you understand that my family needs me here now more than ever."

"Don't you worry about me. I'll just report in early to my new assignment and save my leave time for when we can get together.

How long do you think you'll be staying at home?"

"My boss told me to take all the time I need, but I think that I will probably go back to Washington in about a week. Staying here will just remind me more of losing Dad. At least working will help take my mind off of it for a while during the day."

Once again, the operator interrupted our conversation, requesting an additional deposit of coins.

"Jim, I've got to go with Mama to the church. So call me again when you can.

I love you."

Before I could answer, the dial tone buzzed in my ear.

"Darn phones.

You'd think they could at least give you a warning and let you say goodbye."

CHAPTER SEVENTEEN

An unexpected death is tragic any time of the year, but especially during the Christmas holidays. Helen's father was buried at Meriden's Sacred Heart cemetery on December 22nd. It placed a pall on the entire holiday and would do so for Christmas seasons henceforth for the Brand family.

Despite Helen's family trying to talk her out of returning to Washington so soon, she left on New Year's Day with plans to return to work the following Monday morning, the fourth. The weekend would give her a chance to settle back into her previous routine at the boarding house. And it would give her a chance to sit down and write a nice long letter to me. She wanted to express her feelings to me for my concern for her and her family, and for my phone calls at a crucial time in her life. And for the beautiful flowers that I had sent to the funeral home. She knew that it strained my finances and she wanted me to know just how much she and her family appreciated the sentiment and sacrifice.

At Camp Pendleton things were progressing rapidly as the war entered its third calendar year. It had been only thirteen months, but it already affected the first three years of the 1940's decade. The good news from the Pacific War was the announcement that Japan was beginning the evacuation of Guadalcanal. The Solomon Islands campaign was now listed as a victory for the Allies and the Marines who had fought there were ordered to the Hawaiian Islands for rest and recuperation before another assignment.

I returned to Pendleton after taking a few days of rest in the Los Angeles area. I felt that I deserved a break after working the entire year of nineteen forty-two and then having to suffer through the death of Helen's father from my remote location across the country. I was spent mentally and physically and needed a little time before casting myself headlong into a new endeavor. My CO had encouraged me to take a well deserved leave.

I arrived back at Camp Pendleton ready to delve into my new assignment with the 4th Marines.

My initial duty was preparing things for their arrival which would be in phases as various regimental components that would comprise the 4th came into camp. Then, as they were settled into place, I would assume leadership of a full regiment of the 23rd infantry which was organizing at New River, North Carolina and would proceed to Camp Pendleton no later than July of nineteen forty-three.

When I returned to my barracks, I found a letter from Helen sitting on my bed.

> My Darling Jim,
>
> Well, I'm finally back in Washington after two trying weeks at home. Losing my father has been very hard on all of us as you might well imagine. Although I haven't been home much in recent years, the knowledge that someone is there, even though you can't see them or hear them is comforting. Likewise, knowing that they are no longer there is heart rendering.
>
> Throughout it all, my thoughts were constantly on you.
>
> How I wished that you could have been here to hold me and cheer me up as only you can do. I know that if circumstances were different you would have flown to my side. Through it all, I am glad that you are safe and that thought continues to reassure me.
>
> Things are busier than ever here with the war effort in full swing. I usually don't get home until after six p.m. most days, which is good since it gives me less time to focus on the bad things in both of our lives. When I finally lay down for the night, be

assured that my last thoughts of the day are on you and on our life together after this crazy war is done . . . hopefully soon.

Take care, my darling, and write soon and often.

I love you.

Helen

I sat and reminisced over the words I had just read. I wished I could be more optimistic about her hoping that the war would soon be over. But in my position, I knew that the probability of an early conclusion was virtually impossible. My only wish was for my own safe return from combat and a full and long life together with Helen and any children that might come from our union.

I did my best to keep busy with the primary and collateral duties assigned me by the Marine Corps. In that way, I was able to keep my mind off the perils of war that I knew I would be facing in the near future, and of Helen all alone in Washington, a continent away from my arms.

"Jim, the CO would like to see you ASAP."

"Did he say what it's about?"

"No, but it sounded important."

The commanding officer was Lt. Colonel Samuel C. Hartoon, a native of South Carolina. I had only been under his command for a few weeks and so far liked what I had seen of him.

"Lieutenant Mathews to see the colonel" I said to the staff sergeant in the outer office.

The sergeant smiled and stood and gave me a crisp salute.

"Right this way, sir. The colonel is expecting you."

As I entered the colonel's office, I was surprised to see several of my fellow Marines there. Before I could register too much of a surprise, or say a word, the colonel spoke.

"1st Lieutenant Mathews, I have the honor of presenting you with your new rank insignia and congratulations on a job well done. Since you've been at Pendleton, you and your men have done an excellent job in organizing *things and keeping our troops moving through at a rapid pace. The training has been exemplary and the command felt you should be rewarded for your efforts.*

So, Jim, please accept my 1ˢᵗ Lieutenant bars."

With that, he pinned them onto my collars.

The men all lined up to congratulate me. While I was busy shaking hands, I had two thoughts running through my mind: the need to tell Helen the good news, and the obligation and risk that my new rank gave me when I finally had to go into combat.

The year was passing quickly and July nineteen forty-three arrived along with the 27th regiment, my new outfit. As soon as the command officers arrived, I was prompt to pay my respects. The new CO, Colonel George Smith greeted me heartily.

"Lieutenant Mathews, glad to have you joining us. I hear that you and your men have done an outstanding job with things here. And congratulations on your recent promotion. The way things are going, hopefully we can tack another one on soon."

"Thank you, sir."

"This is Major Bill Tyler, my plans officer; Major John Moffett, my ops officer; and Captain Mason Geary, my logistics officer.

I'm temporarily appointing you as my training officer."

A smile lit up my face I'm sure. I knew that if I did well in this new position that another promotion could be forthcoming very soon. Normal time in rank before promotion was essentially disbanded during war time.

"Yes, sir.

Thank you, sir."

"And Jim, we're not very formal around here during war time. So you're free to use first names when it's only the officers together."

"Thank you, sir . . . er, George."

The colonel smiled in return.

"Now, I'd like a meeting of this entire group and anyone else you deem necessary at 0700 tomorrow. You can brief us on the layout of the camp and plans that are already in progress. Bill and John will in turn update us on our timetable for deployment and our needs while we're still stateside."

∽

So here I was, back in the training division from whence I had come. Plans were nice, but training was the heart of the Marines . . . the "grunts" as we had become known . . . probably because we did the backbreaking work of securing enemy strongholds, be they whole islands or strategic hills or airfields.

The thought of making captain at an early age was appealing, but then there was the responsibility that accompanied it. I was aware of reports emanating from the front lines that it was the junior officers such as lieutenants and captains that were atop the officer casualty lists since they generally led their troops into battle. I hoped that Helen would be proud of my new rank and title when it came . . . although I feared that she would also be aware of the potential hazards that accompanied promotions.

In Washington, things were humming along at the same pace for Helen. She missed me terribly and daily conveyed that to me in her letters. The war effort was progressing favorably according to the news that was broadcast on radio . . . but from what she heard at her work and the vague comments that I allowed, she knew that was probably not the truth. In the U.S., the Japanese succeeded in dropping bombs in a remote part of Oregon and submarines sent two torpedoes into a pier at Santa Barbara. However, both of these events were held secret by the American press at the request of President Roosevelt so as to not unduly alarm the American public.

I had my work cut out for me for the foreseeable future so my men and I got right to the task.

CHAPTER EIGHTEEN

The various regiments that would constitute the 4th Marine Division were now assembled at Camp Pendleton, and the scuttlebutt was that we would soon be sent to the Hawaiian Islands in preparation for action somewhere in the Pacific arena. Nineteen forty-three had seen early victories for the Allies in Burma and New Guinea; a decisive naval battle at Bismarck Sea; and the expulsion of the Japanese from the Aleutian Islands. In April, code breakers pinpointed the location of Admiral Yamamoto. Eighteen P-38 aircraft were dispatched to find him. His plane was sighted and shot down near the Solomon Islands resulting in the Admiral's death.

The 4th had continued its efforts at Camp Pendleton non-stop until finally orders to deploy to Maui on the Hawaiian Islands came. I had been working constantly, and even though Helen and I had debated her coming to California, there was never a time when I could be assured a few days off.

So. It was finally here . . . my time to face up to the war that I had known was coming and that I would have to fight in . . . ever since I had been a recruit at Parris Island.

Though my superiors marked me as a superb soldier and a natural born leader . . . in my heart of hearts I couldn't help but wonder . . . would I measure up when the time came and it mattered most?

Only time would tell . . . and for me that time was getting uncomfortably close.

Finally, the pre-debarkation maneuvers were beginning. My fellow soldiers and I were transported along with other components of the 4th by troop trucks to the Naval Base at Coronado, California, a suburb of the growing port city of San Diego. The facilities there traced their origins to the early 1920's when visionary naval personnel secured the land. Then thanks to the work of (now) Admiral Chester Nimitz and others, it had been turned into a full fledged ship repair facility and debarkation port.

Our mission in the fall of nineteen forty-three was amphibious maneuvers . . . practicing beach landings . . . at Catalina Island and at Pendleton Point, adjacent to our home facility. It seemed like a long time since the amphibious assault training that I had helped lead while training in North Carolina only a few years earlier. I thought back to those days and the Higgins boats, precursor to the more modern landing craft now in use. It would be good to get back into action. Even though my men and I would know that this was only a training exercise, we also knew that it was important to learn all that we could from the experience since it undoubtedly would not be long before we were engaging in the real thing.

The transport ships took us to within a half mile or so of our projected landing sites and then transferred us into the LST's (Landing Ship Transport) that would ferry us to shore.

"Now listen up men, when the ramp opens move as quickly as you can to our rally point on the beach. Stay low and fast and remember that under actual combat conditions the enemy will be trying their damnedest to kill us . . . and that means every one of us. Stay with your buddy and move . . . move . . . move. When we reach the rally point, we'll decide on our next priority objective.

Any questions?"

There was a brief silence followed by a loud "No Sir" in unison.

"All right, then.

Saddle up."

We donned our gear and prepared to move.

The LST's engines ground to a halt as the craft approached the shallow water at beach's edge. The ramps deployed quickly and I gave the order to move. Within thirty seconds my twenty-four Marines and I were in the water and striding onto the beach. The opposition forces (friendly) were firing live ammo over our heads in an effort to simulate real combat.

"Keep low" I shouted.

"Remember the ammo is live. So if you want to live to fight the Japs don't stand up and take a round here. There's no heroism in being killed by your own bullets on your own beach."

The weather was warm and humid, but far less so than I imagined it would be on some remote Pacific island where we might eventually find ourselves struggling to survive. As I debarked and headed for shore, I briefly thought of Helen and all our plans. I tried to imagine what she would be doing at that exact moment and if she might also be thinking of me. I quickly gazed heavenward and said a silent prayer for my safety and the safety of my men whom I was sure were having similar thoughts about their loved ones.

The exercise went well and concluded by the end of the day.

We were transported back to Coronado. The following day we would repeat the exercise, only this time at Pendleton Point . . . and various places again and again until command was sure we were ready for the real thing.

I was right in my assumptions: we practiced the beach assaults over and over until they felt we could perform it in our sleep . . . as well we might eventually have to do.

"But just keep remembering that this is just practice, and no one here is trying to kill you. When we get to the real thing, it'll be man for man. The Japs will be trying to kill us just as much as we'll be trying to kill them."

As much as I wished for the days back in Washington when I kept almost regular hours and knew that I could finish my day with Helen in my arms, I almost longed for a taste of combat. I had joined the Corps knowing of the impending war and had spent all of my time on active duty preparing myself and others for it. Once and for all I needed to prove to myself that I was a man worthy of the title of U.S. Marine; to show my country and myself just what I was made of; to know that my men considered me worthy of being their leader.

On the last day of November the orders finally arrived: we were to proceed to Coronado for immediate departure to the island of Maui in the Hawaiian Islands where we would set up our staging camp. Our ultimate destination(s) would remain unknown until we were en route at which time our CO would announce it to everyone on board at the same time.

"Men, you are about to go into harm's way."

Commodore Byron McCandless was commanding officer of Naval Base, San Diego.

"I know that your training has prepared you for whatever you may encounter in the Pacific theater of war. For those of you in command positions, lead your men with courage. For those of you who must follow, listen to your leaders, do what you are ordered to do with boldness just as you have been trained. Stay tight with your comrades and I know that victory will favor those whose motives are right.

And now, I bid you 'fair winds and following seas'."

I looked around at my men and could see misty eyes everywhere. I had all I could do to control my own emotions on this auspicious occasion. My thoughts as usual were of Helen and all our hopes and dreams for the future. I knew I must find a way to call her one more time before sailing.

Sailing time was set for 0700 the following morning on board the USS J.C. Breckenridge, a former passenger ship that had been converted into a troop transport like many others in her class.

I was able to find a nearby phone booth and armed with a pocketful of quarters, placed a call to Helen at her boarding house.

She was already in tears when she came to the phone.

"How are you, my darling?"

"Oh Jim, I've been so worried about you.

Are you still in the states?

I was so afraid that you wouldn't have a chance to call me once you got to San Diego."

I had written her before leaving Camp Pendleton and updated her on my tentative schedule.

"We set sail to Hawaii in the morning. That should have us there in about a week. After that, well your guess is as good as mine. They purposefully keep us in the dark about our destinations until we're en route. That reduces chances of anyone inadvertently telling someone who might accidentally tip off the wrong person. We don't need the enemy knowing any more of our business than necessary.

This new radar I told you about is letting us know about aircraft movements like never before, and it won't be long until everyone will have it. But, enough about me. How are you and what's new in D.C.?"

"I'm fine and the family is fine. My work stays about the same, so at least part of the day my thoughts are occupied with matters other than worrying about you . . . but only for short periods of time."

"Helen, you've got to have positive thoughts. I'm planning on surviving the war and coming home to you . . . to marrying you and having a family as we've planned.

So you've got to be thinking the same way."

"Jim, I'm trying . . . but it's not easy. Every day we hear reports from overseas, and they're not very encouraging . . . especially from the Pacific."

I could hear her muffled sobs and could imagine the tears flowing down her cheeks.

"No matter what happens, know that I love you and always will love you. And I'm planning on fulfilling my promise to you to return."

We whispered sweet nothings until the operator interrupted asking for additional money.

"I'd better go. My men and I have a lot to do before we deploy in the morning.

I love you, Helen."

"I love you, Jim."

The phone suddenly went dead.

I stood there for a moment, gathered my thoughts and headed back to my men and our rendezvous with destiny.

Chapter Nineteen

The convoy of ships set sail promptly at 0700. Within an hour we were out of sight of land headed into the deep blue waters of the Pacific Ocean. Hawaii lay approximately twenty-five hundred miles southwest of the southern California coast.

The first two days were uneventful, but as we were approaching the mid-portion of the journey, the seas roughened considerably. Word from the quarterdeck was that we were heading into a typhoon . . . a Pacific hurricane. I still had not gotten my sea legs, nor had most of my men. I spent most of my time along with them confined to my bunk or leaning over the side rails retching my guts out.

"Lieutenant, I didn't think officers were supposed to get sea sick."

I turned toward one of my men who had joined me on deck.

"There's nothing in the military regs that I know of that says that. I wish it were true however. I've never been to sea before. Arkansas doesn't have any open waters like this."

"The storm appears to be subsiding a bit, sir. If we can just hold on a few more days."

"At least the fresh air makes me feel a little better. The heat and smell below deck doesn't help."

"No, sir."

On the sixth day at sea, the outline of the Hawaiian Islands came into view and everyone on board rejoiced at the thought of putting their feet onto dry, stationary land, albeit not knowing how long it might be before we set sail again for a destination that would surely thrust us into harm's way.

The island of Maui was majestic in the distance. The weather was clear as we approached the shore. In the distance we could see the summit of Mt. Haleakala, although we didn't know it by name. A circle of clouds rimmed the peak about half way up its base. The line of ships navigated westward past Lahaina, the old whaling capital of the Pacific. In days long gone, whale blubber yielded precious oil to fuel lamps. Then the convoy turned eastward along the north shore to the docks at Kahalui, situated adjacent to an old airfield that had been renovated and was now in use by the U.S. Army Aircorps.

By early afternoon the ships were moored safely and our troops began disembarking. As soon as the jeeps and troop carriers had been off loaded, convoys formed up for the relatively short trip to "Camp Maui" as it came to be called. How the camp came into the possession of the 4th Marines was the subject of many stories. Some said it had been made for the Army originally, but they would have none of it, which made it perfect for the Marines. Some said it was situated in a location to simulate the tropic conditions of the Pacific islands that the Marines would soon be fighting for. Whatever the truth, it was situated fifteen hundred feet up on the side of the world's largest extinct volcano, Haleakala.

The weather on Haleakala was a meteorological freak of nature. Rain clouds that passed over its crest descended to lower warmer levels where they dumped their moisture. The rain cascaded down to the lower levels of the mountain side, often in torrents, creating mud that often was so deep it plucked boots right off the feet of soldiers. There was an old story circulating there that told of a Marine who lost a boot, but wasn't aware of it for three days. He would just sit down at night and unlace the mud and put it back on again the following morning.

As soon as our tent city had been erected, I took out pen and paper and began a letter to Helen. It had already been over a week since I had spoken to her and I knew she would be anxious to know that I had arrived safely. For now I wrote that I was fine, that the trip over had been tolerable, although "I still feel like I'm at sea even though I've been on dry land for almost two days. The Hawaiian Islands are beautiful, but the humidity here is worse than Washington, D.C. in mid-summer, and it's almost Christmas time." I also explained about the weather patterns and Mt. Haleakala.

"So far, no word about when we might go back to sea and where they might send us. As I mentioned before, they don't tell us where we're going until we're at sea. That way we can't tell our loved ones where we'll be when word starts coming about casualties at a particular location."

I went on to tell her of my love and that my thoughts were on her constantly and closed as always with a short prayer that I would return safely to her so that we could fulfill all our dreams and plans. As I placed the letter into the envelope, I wept silently. In my heart of hearts, I was becoming more fearful that those dreams would never come to pass.

Christmas was beautiful in the tropics, albeit very lonely. The troops longed to be home with their loved ones instead of being constantly poised for war; the ever present realization that we might never make it home alive . . . never get to hold our loved ones again . . . never get to spend a Christmas the old fashioned way pervaded our thoughts. The Marines were provided a turkey and ham dinner, but it wasn't the same as homemade and it didn't seem quite right with the temperatures hovering in the low eighties.

Then there were the letters from home. While everyone appreciated hearing from loved ones at this time of the year, somehow it just made it all the more lonely. I sat and read . . . and reread . . . several letters I received from Helen the day before Christmas. While she always included news from home, and summarized things at work, she always reminisced about our time together before I departed for California and of our hopes and dreams for the future . . . all of which just added to my loneliness and longing for her and for home. It was also a time of sad remembrance of the passing of her father just a year earlier and the trip to California that never happened.

Shortly after the New Year nineteen forty-four was ushered in, scuttlebutt began circulating that several battalions of the 4th would be deployed to the first major assault of the division's many campaigns to come . . . Roi-Namur Island. The island held an airfield occupied by the Japanese and it needed to be recaptured in order to eliminate a strategic air base of the enemy. The island was the northern most part of the Kwajalein atoll in the Marshall Island chain. As it turned out, the battle was intense but thankfully short lasting less than a week . . . but it was costly nevertheless. The Marines had learned their lessons from previous island battles and this time invaded both from the north and south ends of the atoll. Over forty thousand U.S. troops bottled up the eighty-one hundred Japanese troops who occupied the island and in a little over three days eliminated all but about two hundred and fifty of them.

As the troops who had been engaged there returned to Maui, stories of the horrors of battle began to circulate. The Japanese had earned a reputation for their viciousness in war . . . and the stories told by the men who had been there confirmed it. Many of the dead Marines had been beheaded or otherwise mutilated by the enemy. Dozens of Korean laborers who worked for the Japanese were found with their hands and feet bound and their throats slit.

I heard the stories along with the others who had not been there and pushed them into the deep recesses of my mind. This was something that I definitely would not be mentioning to Helen in a letter. My hope was that the media was not focusing on it in radio briefs about the war or in the Movietone films that were played in theaters prior to the featured film.

After the victory in the Marshall Islands came additional captures at Truk in the Caroline Islands, destruction of the Japanese air base at Rabaul near Papua, New Guinea and air attacks on the Mariana Islands.

By late May, the 4th received orders to proceed into the western Pacific. On board we received our destination: Saipan. Pre-invasion bombardment began on June 13th with deliverance of over one hundred eighty-five thousand shells by seven new battleships and additional shelling the following day by eight older battleships and eleven cruisers that were more accurate in their placement. On June fifteenth, more than three hundred LVT's landed eight thousand Marines on the west coast of Saipan by 0900.

The invasion surprised the Japanese high command who expected the forces to land much farther south. Admiral Toyoda Soemu, commander-in-chief of the Japanese Navy saw an opening to use his A-go readiness forces to attack the ships stationed around the island; but, the resulting Battle of the Philippine Sea was a disaster for their navy which lost three carriers and hundreds of planes.

While I had been a distant participant, staying at sea and helping with plans, I began to get my first taste of actual combat and saw the results first hand of the sorts of injuries the Japanese were capable of inflicting on American troops. And the Americans too showed our necessary ruthlessness by the use of flamethrowers to clear caves and liberal use of machine guns to repel charges by the suicide divisions of Japanese who had decided that they would not surrender or be taken alive as the battle waned in favor of the U.S.

When fighting was officially declared over on July 9th, over thirty thousand Japanese lay dead. The U.S. toll, while one of the highest of the war so far at almost three thousand, was only one tenth that of the enemy.

I set sail along with my men in mid-July westward in the Pacific to the small island known as Tinian, a part of the Marianas chain along with Guam and Saipan. The former had been under aerial attack along with the other islands in the chain since early February of nineteen forty four, and the latter had just been secured earlier in the same month. Word was that other troops had invaded the island of Guam on the nineteenth following what came to be known as the "Mariana's Turkey Shoot" . . . occurring in the third week of June; carrier based U.S. fighters shot down over two hundred enemy aircraft while losing only twenty.

The battle was mercifully short, lasting just over a week. It marked the first time that U.S. aircraft had dropped napalm, used to clear away foliage and expose the enemy battlements. The campaign was a resounding U.S. victory with over eight thousand Japanese casualties compared to three hundred and twenty-eight Marines.

The C.O., Colonel Harry Schmidt, told me that I had led my men brilliantly during the first eight days of battle. Now, however, we found ourselves at the bottom of a ridge where resistance was still apparent. Colonel

Schmidt sent word that the operation was wrapping up, but the few final holdouts needed to be taken.

We prepared for a final "suicide attack" by the remaining garrison atop the hill. Like Saipan before it, the remaining Japanese troops had refused to be taken alive.

"Here they come. We'd better fix bayonets just in case."

The mortarmen leveled their weapons onto the hillside as the Japs came spilling over the ridge and down the embankment toward us.

"Keep spraying them with that thirty cal, and reset your aim with those mortars. You're overshooting them by at least twenty yards."

The result was devastating to the enemy. They ran into the face of bullets and shells aimed right at their center mass, taking them down by the dozens with each round of fire. Abruptly, just at it had begun, all movement stopped.

"Cease fire, boys," I yelled to my troops.

Suddenly, all was quiet.

I ordered my first sergeant to scramble up the hill and inspect the enemy's bunker. Sergeant Norman and his men carefully climbed the embankment and made their way to the bunker. Just to be safe, he lobbed a grenade into it, but there was no response.

"All clear, sir" he yelled from the top of the ridge.

I climbed my way up to the top and inspected the bunker.

"Sergeant, notify Colonel Schmidt that the island is secure."

"Yes, sir," he said with a crisp salute.

"Boys, let's wrap it up, and join our comrades at headquarters. It's time we got back to Maui."

Amidst the cheering of the squads of men, our troops made their way back through the throngs of dead bodies of the fallen enemy. I stopped aside one of the dead. In the soldier's pocket was a small booklet containing the picture of a lovely young Japanese woman holding a small child.

"That could just as easily be Helen holding our child someday.

Lord, may I never be the one lying on the ground with an enemy soldier looking at my family's picture."

I looked heavenward, bowed my head and said a short prayer.

The return trip to Maui gave us a chance to relax from the rigors of war, but for all of us . . . the experienced fighters and the first timers . . . the *visions of the horrors that were created by us and the enemy would linger in our memories for years to come . . . and in some until the day they died.*

The seas were relatively calm so seasickness was at a minimum. Mail was still a luxury that would await us upon our return to the Hawaiian Islands.

When we finally reached homeport, things had changed for the better. The rains had subsided for the time being and the mud had dried. New tents with wooden flooring had been erected and electric lighting had been installed. The following day mail call brought extra sacks of mail that had been awaiting us. There were fifteen letters from Helen. I retired to my bunk where I could be alone while I read Helen's words.

> *"Dear Jim,*
>
> *I pray that when you read this letter you will be safe and sound back in the Hawaiian Islands, out of harm's way. I miss you so much every day, all day and all night long. I know that I am in your thoughts too and that sustains me for now.*
>
> *But I continue to dream of the day when we will be together again and can do all the things that we planned.*
>
> *My work here continues much the same every day. Since I am working with the government, I can't help but hear about what is going on in the Pacific area. I am heartened by reports that things seem to be turning in favor of the U.S. Some say that the war could be over in a year or less. President Roosevelt seems optimistic at times. I'm sure that the war in Europe and in the Pacific is wearing on him. Recent pictures of him are not flattering. He appears to have aged twenty years since Pearl Harbor.*
>
> *I hope to hear from you soon. Know that you have my love forever."*
>
> *Helen*

I just sat there and contemplated her words, then continued with the other letters that conveyed similar sentiments. I almost cried as I read and reread her heartfelt words of love. I knew I had to survive the war and get home to her safely.

❧

The fall of nineteen forty-four was relatively peaceful for the 4th Marines. We were able to recover from our assault on Tinian and then prepare for whatever else might be thrown at us in the coming months. My men and I reveled at the news coming in from the war front. In successive months, the capture of the Marianas was completed, the Navy posted a major defeat of the Japanese at the battle of Leyte Gulf, American B-29s successfully bombed the Nakajima aircraft factory near Tokyo and word was that the U.S. was preparing a new secret weapon that could be used on Japan to end the war.

Early nineteen forty-five saw the appointment of General Douglas MacArthur as commander of all ground forces and Admiral Chester Nimitz as commander of naval forces for the upcoming invasion of Iwo Jima, Okinawa and Japan itself.

By the end of January, nineteen forty-five it was obvious to the 4th that something big was coming our way. Supply ships had been unloading tons of ordnance and foodstuffs and water in preparation for transfer to the assault ships that would take us to our destination. The Marines were gearing up for another amphibious assault with daily practices carried out on the shores of Molokai, Lanai and even the rugged northeast coast of Maui.

My letters to Helen were becoming more frequent as I tried to assuage my fears of the impending campaign, yet all the while assuring her that I would return safely to her.

CHAPTER TWENTY

Muddy or not, Maui was a little piece of heaven to the fatigued and sea weary men. The improvements . . . new tents, wooden ramps that allowed our troops to move about without getting stuck in the mud, and electricity giving us lights and hot water for the first time since our arrival months earlier made our lives a little more comfortable. Many of the roads were now paved with wooden logs giving our little tropical paradise an aura reminiscent of some towns in the old west.

I was sitting in my tent reading a letter from Helen when a stranger appeared in the doorway. I glanced up and noticed that he wore 2nd lieutenant bars and was from the 3rd Marines.

"What can I help you with, Lieutenant?"

He entered slowly, saluted crisply and identified himself.

"Second Lieutenant David Peterman, sir.

I just returned from Guam, sir. Our detachment had been acting as a police squad guarding the airfield after our victory there. Many of us from the 3rd are now assigned to your unit. Looks like something big is cooking. No one will say for sure, but it's bound to be one of the islands closer to Japan that has an airfield. We need something closer to Tokyo to launch our planes."

"Jim Mathews, Lieutenant.

Glad to make your acquaintance. And you can skip the formalities here."

We shook hands.

"So, what's your preference, David or Dave?"

"Dave's fine."

"Where are you from, Dave? With a name like that I'm going to guess the Midwest somewhere."

"Pretty good guess. My home town is Oconto Falls, Wisconsin. It's just north of Green Bay. But then, I'm sure you never heard of it. Population less than a thousand."

"No. Can't say I'm familiar with either one. Milwaukee's the only name that comes to mind . . . beer capital of the world, isn't it?"

"Great town . . . bar on every corner and you can get a big glass of beer for a nickel.

How about you, Jim? Where are you from?"

"Grew up in a small town in Arkansas, not too far from Little Rock. Didn't like it much, so I welcomed the opportunity to get away when some folks invited me to join them on a visit to a Marine Corps recruiter station. I liked what I heard, and as they say . . . the rest is history. Of course I wasn't expecting to wind up out here even though it was obvious since around the time I graduated high school that something bad was brewing in the world. But I guess I was expecting Europe, since I assumed that's where the action would be."

"From what I hear from my brother . . . he's in the Army in George Patton's division in France . . . it ain't no picnic there either. For all the hot and humid weather we've had here, they're having to fight in sub-zero temperatures most of the time. He was lucky not to have been at Normandy . . . that's got to be one of the worst days of the war for our troops."

I nodded my agreement.

"So, how was it out there?"

"Pretty bad. Over six hundred from my outfit KIA and over three thousand injured. But capturing the airfield on Guam is helping the fight in the Pacific. Those new B-29s have a much better range. They've been able to raid Tokyo and several other key cities in Japan."

"So I've been told. I hear they took out an airplane manufacturing plant in Nakajima."

"Yep. Heard that too" Dave replied.

"Got a family?"

"No, just my folks at home and a younger sister in high school. My brother is just a year older than me."

"Girlfriend or fiancée?"

"Had one when the war started. But she just couldn't stand the waiting and not knowing what might happen to me. Married one of my best friends and already a baby on the way.

What about you?"

I smiled as I thought about Helen.

"Yep."

I took out the only picture I had of her, showing us together in Washington, D.C.

"Quite a looker" he commented.

"Engaged?"

"Right after I finished OCS and before I got sent to the West coast. She's from Connecticut, but works in Washington for the former mayor of her town. We're planning on tying the knot just as soon as this damn war is over."

"You're lucky to have someone back home to worry about you like I'm betting she does."

I held up the stack of letters that I'd been reading.

"I only get an occasional one from my folks. Mom's not much on writing and when she does you can hear the tears in her words . . . she's so concerned that I won't make it home. And to be honest with you, I'm not so sure I will either."

I looked at him and just nodded. No words could assuage the thought that was pervasive on the minds of every Marine and soldier in combat.

I hadn't had a friend I could easily confide in for a long time. Dave had a manner about him that was agreeable from our first meeting. He showed genuine concern for my background and interests but without prying too deeply into obviously personal affairs. He had the knack of knowing when to stop . . . when the question on his mind was too personal. He seemed to instinctively know that in due time I would confide in him if I cared to share whatever had been on my mind. I thought back over my time in the military and couldn't find anyone who had instilled this feeling in me before.

In fact, with the exception of Helen, I couldn't remember anyone in my life that matched Dave in that regard.

Friends in the military are hard to come by. Perhaps it's because of the frequent moves that are constantly separating people. Or, especially during war time, the fact that close friends can be taken away from you permanently . . . suddenly . . . by a bullet or some other equally lethal device.

The winds of war continued to blow. Things in the Pacific campaign continued to indicate that the U.S. and her allies were slowly but steadily pushing the Japanese back toward her homeland. And in Europe, too, the push was on to force Hitler to abandon his ill-gotten gains in France and the intervening countries between there and the Fuhrer's hometown, Berlin.

MacArthur and Nimitz were in control in the Pacific theater and it looked as though their tactics were working. And on Maui, preparations were underway for the next island assault by the 4ᵗʰ Marines. We didn't know it yet, but our target was a small dot on the map, a member of the Volcano Islands chain called Iwo Jima.

Original 1944 planning map for the invasion of Iwo Jima from the author's private collection.

CHAPTER TWENTY-ONE

The island of Iwo Jima, a part of the archipelago known as the Volcano Islands, lies strategically about six hundred and fifty miles south of Tokyo, Japan. It was originally chartered as Sulphur Island by Captain James Cook on his third surveying voyage in seventeen seventy-nine. The Japanese traditionally knew it as Iwotso; jima was an alternative pronunciation for to, *the Japanese word for island. Japanese naval officers sent to fortify it mistakenly referred to it as Iwo Jima, the less popular name, thus making it the mainstream name that it came to be known by during the famous battle that occurred there.*

In size, it is diminutive at just eight square miles. Despite being volcanic in origin, it is remarkably flat except for the peak, Mt. Suribachi, at its southern tip. The latter rises only five hundred and twenty-eight feet above sea level. The flattened portions of the island were perfect for the construction of runways and the Japanese had built several there. Planes launched from these fields had been responsible for harrying U.S. bombers en route to Tokyo. The U.S. military needed to take the island both to prevent further action against their aircraft by Japanese fighters stationed there, and to have a place to launch aircraft during the invasion of Japan, already in the planning stages.

Despite its size, during the battle that took place there from February 19, 1945 until March 26, 1945, it was the most densely populated place on earth, having more residents per square mile than even Manhattan Island in New York City.

❧

By the end of January, nineteen forty-five preparations for our next deployment were in full gear. I had gathered my troops together for the announcement they all feared was coming.

"We get under way day after tomorrow. All I can tell you now is that we'll be sailing west again to another island in the Pacific that MacArthur and Nimitz want and need. We've got to control the islands with air fields since they're sending out planes to intercept our bombers and are killing our pilots in record numbers as they attempt to hit mainland Japan. Our current fields are too far out for the aircraft that are currently in use. And command knows that we're just the ones that can do the job.

So let's get it done and soon we'll be sailing back to mainland U.S. and to our homes and wives and sweethearts.

Semper Fi!"

The group erupted with "Semper Fi" in response.

❧

Dave came over to me after the troops had dispersed.

"It must be tough to be in charge and have to do something like that."

I looked pensively in Dave's direction.

"You'll get your chance . . . probably sooner than you like. And when it comes, I know you'll be ready for it. Now, I've got a letter to write before we ship out."

That was my signal that I wanted my privacy and Dave instinctively turned and left me alone.

"Dear Helen,

We are about to sail again. I can't tell you exactly where we are going since I don't know myself. All I know and can say is that it is somewhere west of here.

119

The Japanese know by now that they are steadily losing the war, but their traditions won't let them acknowledge it publicly. So they're prepared to fight to the end and that will mean a lot of unnecessary deaths on both sides.

You know that I will do everything in my power to be one of those who survives this horrible thing called war. I made a promise to you and I intend to keep it. I want to return to you so that we can do all the things we talked about: getting married, having a family and living out our lives together.

I pray every day that the Almighty will guide my steps so that when the war is over I may do just that.

Keep me in your prayers in the coming weeks and months and try not to let any bad news coming from the front upset you unduly. It may be difficult for me to communicate with you for quite a while, so keep fond thoughts of me in your heart as I do of you in mine.

Always,

Jim

The convoy of ships made its way from the docks at Kahalui into the open seas west of Maui. The late winter months were known for their rough seas and the year nineteen forty-five did not disappoint. Men stayed in their bunks or hung over the side rails on the windswept decks when forced to be topside.

"Good morning, Lieutenant" the captain of the bridge greeted me heartily.

"Good morning, Captain Loving" I replied in turn. Loving was a naval lieutenant commander, but was entitled to the "captain" greeting as commanding officer on board.

"I'm now authorized to tell you that our destination is the island of Iwo Jima in the Volcano Island chain. I think you know of it already since it is close to Saipan and Tinian Islands where you Marines have been in the past year."

"Yes, sir. I was a part of the Tinian campaign. I've heard plenty about Iwo Jima . . . kind of figured that's where we were heading. Scuttlebutt is that there are airfields on the island that the brass needs. It'll put us a lot closer to the Japanese mainland."

"Sounds like someone in the know has been shooting off at the mouth. You seem to have a grasp of the situation, so spread the word to your men. Our sailing time should be just a little over two weeks."

I gathered my men together and performed the onerous task knowing that other squadron commanders were doing the same as I spoke.

"It's Iwo Jima" I said in a firm voice and then rested long enough for it to sink in.

"Our sailing time is about two weeks, so plan on d-day to be on or about the nineteenth of this month. As we get closer, command will be able to firm that up. It's a small island, but the Japanese own it, we want it and they know it . . . and they'll throw everything they've got at us to keep us from getting it. The destroyers leading the task force along with our aircraft will do all they can to soften it up before the actual invasion, but our enemy is tough as we all know from previous encounters with them. So prepare your gear and yourselves accordingly. We'll have briefings as we get closer and update you on the progress of the pre-assault shelling.

Any questions?"

The men were strangely quiet. Like me, they had heard the rumors and once more the thought of going up against the Japanese put fright into their every thought. Word was that the enemy soldiers knew they were losing and national pride wouldn't allow them to surrender; so, they were fighting with a fatalistic attitude and did things that sane men wouldn't do. The men had heard that the Japanese pilots were engaging in something called "kamikaze" or suicide tactics in which they would dive directly into a ship on purpose, knowing they would be killed in the effort.

"Crazy bastards" I thought to myself. But then we had been through this before and the same thought undoubtedly ran through each of our minds:

"Will I make it back this time?"

After a few moments, I dismissed them and returned to my quarters. I was scared and I knew that my men were too. But they were Marines . . . and Marines always do their duty no matter what.

Curtis LeMay, the American bomber commander in the Pacific theater of war had been planning air raids from Saipan ever since the island had been wrested from the Japanese in the summer of the preceding year. But the island of Iwo Jima held strategic airfields from which the enemy launched fighter squadrons against the U.S. aircraft and against the facility on Saipan itself. Even American sorties that didn't approach the island were detected by radar and reported to mainland Japan. The enemy would then have a two hour warning to prepare for the approaching aircraft.

Iwo had to be taken.

The Japanese high command knew that the invasion was imminent and appointed one of their finest leaders, General Tadamichi Kuribayashi, to be the commander of their forces on Iwo Jima. He had studied traditional Japanese tactics that initially involved attempting to stop invaders on the beaches . . . but almost always failed. This was generally followed by "banzai charges" that resulted in a significant loss of men and resources. He had also studied the plan devised by Lt. General Sadae Inoue, used at the battle of Peleliu, which concentrated on a war of attrition to wear down the enemy. He adopted this strategy for use in the upcoming invasion.

Most importantly he ordered the fortification of the island with the most elaborate system of tunnels ever constructed. Caves, pill boxes, gun emplacements, bunkers, command posts and even hospitals were placed underground and reinforced with heavy steel doors that rendered them impervious to even the most deadly bombing attacks of the campaign. Land mines, "spigot mortars" and well camouflaged firing positions left no place on the island safe from Japanese fire. The interconnecting design of the tunnels allowed passage of troops and supplies from almost any part of the complex to any other without exposing themselves to surface fighting.

Intelligence data prior to the commencement of Operation Detachment (the battle for Iwo Jima) caused the commander of the Fleet Marine Forces Pacific, Lt. General Holland Smith to conclude:

"I don't know who he is (General Kuribayashi), but the Japanese General running this show is one smart bastard."

We sailed to Eniwetok atoll where we stayed for two days; then four days later we docked briefly in Saipan where we received our allotment of munitions and rations before debarking to our final destination, Iwo

Jima. The island in the Northern Marianas group was approximately the same distance to Iwo Jima as the latter was to Tokyo. Since its capture in the summer of ninety forty-four, it had been important as a launch point to intercept enemy aircraft en route to Japan. We were still several days steaming time to our rendezvous point off the coast of Iwo Jima, but already word was coming in that Naval forces, both ship and aircraft launched from carriers, were pounding the island preparatory to the ground invasion.

Unknown to the Marines was the fact that Major General Harry Schmidt had requested a full ten days of shelling but was turned down by Admiral Hill "due to insufficient time for the craft to rearm before D-Day." It was finally whittled down to three days, two of which were hampered by inclement weather. In addition, during the second day as underwater frogmen were reconnoitering the beaches, all twelve gunboats that were support screen for them along with the ships USS Pensacola and USS Leutze were hit by fire from the shore batteries.

Admiral Ray Spruance, who had assumed command of the Pacific Fleet during Halsey's illness, was heard to comment on the situation to General Schmidt.

"I know that your people will get away with it."

These words would ring tragically hollow as the fight for the island unfolded.

At 0200 on the morning of February 19, 1945 the shelling began in earnest. The invasion task force had been joined by Task Force fifty-eight under Admiral Marc Mitscher giving a combined total of sixteen aircraft carriers, eight battleships and fifteen cruisers as well as Spruance's flagship, the USS Indianapolis. The sixteen inch guns of the USS North Carolina, USS West Virginia and USS Washington began the assault aided by all the other ships in the fleet using their main guns as well as anti-aircraft weapons and unguided rockets. Refloated battleships from the Pearl Harbor attack including New York, Arkansas, Texas, Idaho, Nevada and Tennessee aimed their deadly cargo at the island. The naval assault was soon followed by over one hundred bombers and a second wave by naval forces.

US forces were soon to learn that the pre-invasion bombardment did little harm to the Japanese armament due to the mostly underground fortification building that had been employed. But the Japanese under

Admiral Kuribayashi knew they were in for a fight that they ultimately could not win.

∽

At 0859, one minute ahead of schedule, the Marines launched their LVTs toward the beaches, landing the first of some thirty thousand troops of the 3rd, 4th and 5th Divisions that would eventually be deployed onto the island. The troop carriers were well armed with seventy-five mm howitzers and three machine guns each.

As they approached the sandy volcanic ash that made up the perimeter of the island, they were stymied by fifteen foot high terraces of the soft material, despite having been assured by the invasion planners from samples returned by the frogmen that it would present only a "minor obstacle". Within short order, dozens of craft and thousands of Marines were stuck on the beaches and hindered from progressing inland. Scouting parties that had advanced found little resistance for quite some distance and concluded that the pre-invasion bombardment had neutralized most of the Japanese positions. Meanwhile, bulldozers aided by "Marston matting" were working furiously to get the troops and equipment beyond the terraces as LVTs and Higgins boats were being damaged by the extreme surf and undertow on the steep beaches.

It was at this point that Admiral Kuribayashi advanced his plan. Instead of waiting until the Marines had reached air field one on the southern portion of the island to begin his full assault, he ordered his forces to open fire on the densely populated beaches where the men were relatively unprotected.

All hell broke loose late that morning. As one battalion commander commented:

"You could have held up a cigarette and lit it on the stuff going by."

CHAPTER TWENTY-TWO

By 0800 my men and I were scrambling over the side of the Breckenridge and making our way down into the LVT's that would ferry us onto the shores of Iwo Jima and into harm's way. Each of the craft held approximately thirty-six men and their armor. Fortunately, after bad weather the day before, skies had cleared and the seas were fairly calm. We were to invade the east coast between Mt. Suribachi and the East Boat Basin. The landing area was divided into seven sectors, each approximately five hundred and fifty yards wide.

Moments before our boats revved up and headed for their landing sites, explosions began on land from ordnance being fired from the USS Texas stationed off the West coast of the island and the USS New York to the east. We all gave out a yell when we heard the shells finding their targets, hoping it would make our approach a little easier and a lot safer.

At precisely 0845, the LVTs began their short hop to the sandy shores that awaited them. The first craft opened its landing door at 0859 and the battle for Iwo Jima had officially begun. Marines sprung into action and waded *ashore and began the climb onto the volcanic sandy shores. Overhead the sky was filled with fighter planes delivering their ordnance onto the hidden enemy inland as well as along the beaches and Mt. Suribachi.*

"Alright men, this is it.

Our landing sector is Red Beach 2 and our objective is to get to airfield No.1.

Just remember, get off the beaches as soon as you can. If you stay there, the Japanese will surely kill you. It's the most vulnerable place of all.

So move! move! move!

I'll see you at our rendezvous point near the airfield."

"This shit is going to be hard to get across" one Marine of the 1st Battalion, 27th Regiment said as his boots became planted deep into the soil.

"Kind of reminds me of the story of the 'mud boots' back in Maui."

Wave after wave of Marines followed along with heavy duty equipment to help in leveling the volcanic ash and clear the way for the men to move inland and gain their objectives. By 1000, however, a traffic jam had become apparent on the beaches. Almost six thousand troops had been deposited on the shores of the tiny island, but the high terraces of volcanic ash had prohibited the men from moving off the beaches as had been planned. As a consequence, men were having to wade in from distances farther out than originally planned and were being dragged under water by the severe undertow so prevalent around the island. Before the day was over, dozens of men drowned due to the heavy packs they carried rendering them unable to overcome the currents.

And all the while, the beaches remained quiet.

One of my men looked at me and asked: "What do you think, Lieutenant? Did the advance shelling take out all of their guns? Do you suppose they abandoned the island over night since they knew we were coming?"

I thought for a minute.

"Corporal, I'd love to think that was the case, but you know the Japanese just aren't known as a race that accepts defeat easily. Unfortunately, they don't believe in retreating. It's a matter of honor to them. They would rather die than suffer those humiliations."

The look on the corporal's face indicated an understanding of my message . . . albeit it was obvious that he didn't much like what he had heard.

"Now, let's get off this damn beach before things liven up." I whispered a few lines of the 23rd psalm as we scrambled toward our objective.

❧

It was almost 1100 and things continued to get more jammed up. The bulldozers were starting to make a little progress leveling the terraces that were the major obstacles to the Marines getting off the beachhead and moving inland.

I had just instructed my men to move when the corporal standing next to me suddenly fell to the ground. I looked down only to find him dead with a bullet wound through the center of his forehead. Instantly, all hell broke loose as machine gun fire and mortar attacks began in earnest.

"Hit the deck . . . incoming" I yelled as I surveyed my men. Already I could see that several members of my unit were down as well as countless others belonging to other units to the left and right of us. The entire beach erupted into one big shooting gallery. Most of the firing was coming from sites at various heights up and down the volcanic peak, Mt. Suribachi. In addition, mortars were being lobbed at us from sites directly in front of us where our objective, the airfield, stood.

"Move forward men" I continued to yell. My counterparts to the left and right were all yelling the same to their men. As we attempted to gain ground inland, the numbers of Marines that were hit by enemy fire began to mount at a staggering rate.

"Medic" reverberated along the beach as the Navy corpsmen stationed with the Marines sought to aid the wounded only to be gunned down themselves by the now continuous stream of bullets and ordnance fragments that rained down on them.

The high berm of sand that had been created by the bulldozers in their effort to clear the beaches now provided cover for the men who were fortunate enough to be near it. The majority of us were caught in the crossfire coming now from all sides and we had precious little protection from the onslaught. The troops that had initially made it past the high sandy terraces had also encountered mine fields that had stopped their advance and added to the quickly mounting list of casualties.

To the right of my unit, elements of the 5th Marines were successful in penetrating the first line of bunkers and pillboxes as one of their group displayed courage typical of the corps when he singlehandedly took out five of them armed with only a pistol and hand grenades before he was killed by a grenade blast himself.

With the lull in firing that occurred with the Marine's action, I and my unit and several adjacent units were able to scramble off the beach to near our objective, Airfield No.1. Tanks were able to move in and help our advance. At the other end of the island, the 28th regiment of the 5th Marines encountered equally heavy resistance as they attempted to take Suribachi. Casualties were high but by late afternoon, elements of the 5th reached the west coast at the base of the mountain.

Meanwhile, on the east side things were not going well. While some Marine units were able to approach the airfield, increasing resistance from additional fortifications along the perimeter of the airstrip kept them pinned down where they were. Numerous squads from my group and other regiments of the 4th and 5th divisions had attempted to move inland only to be decimated by the fury of the machine guns and mortars being thrown at us. The casualty rate continued to rise and by the time darkness had settled over us, it was estimated that there were over twenty-four hundred casualties.

And as day became night, the Japanese continued their constant barrage against our troops making progress all but impossible. We would need the light of day to assess the damage that had been incurred and rework our strategy for obtaining our objectives.

Finally, just around midnight it became quiet. I sought a brief rest while several of my men took turns as lookouts.

"The Japs are known to never rest, so keep an eye out for any motion and keep your ears tuned to any unusual sounds. If you see or hear anything out of the ordinary, report it to me right away."

I took off my helmet and placed it under my head as a pillow stretching out under a coconut tree. Before sleep finally came, my thoughts were on Helen. I imagined her in my arms and could hear her sweet voice responding to me as we prepared to make love.

"Lieutenant, one of the men reports some noises coming from the northeast sector."

I looked at my watch. I had been asleep for just over an hour.

"Alert the men. Who's got our field phone? We need to let the other sectors know about a possible attack."

Before I could secure my helmet in place, the machine guns opened up again striking the sergeant a few yards to my left. He hit the ground with a fury.

"Get those guns over there and give it all you've got" I yelled.

"Gimme that phone. This is Mathews, sector 165. We're taking heavy fire from just to our northeast . . . estimate sector 182 . . . We need some rounds put in there."

"Can do" was the response from the other end of the phone.

"Keep your heads down men. The shelling should start any minute."

Within two or three minutes the sound of incoming shells whizzed overhead and the night sky lit up as they found their mark.

"Good shooting" I reported via phone.

We could use some into sector 183 as well."

Before I could return to my vantage point, additional shells screamed overhead and struck to the east of the first rounds. As the incoming ceased, all was suddenly quiet again.

"I think you got the bastards. You can hold for now" I yelled into the field phone.

"Reset the watch" I yelled to my men as I layed back down and resumed my thoughts of Helen.

The following day dawned wet and windy, making additional landings hazardous due to the high waves and increasingly severe undertow.

On land, Sherman tanks had been deployed to the base of Suribachi and continued their assault on the Japanese artillery along the rim of the mountain while providing cover for the 5th Division. To the east, the 4th Marines moved toward the Quarry, another of their objectives, aided by shelling from the USS Washington and by the Navy Construction Battalion (Seabees) and their heavy duty equipment that removed debris in their way and provided cover as they advanced.

The 25th regiment had been ordered to hold what they could while they advanced alongside their fellow Marines towards their mutual objectives, Airfields 1 & 2 and the Quarry.

I and my men, while not exactly the most battle hardened troops in the field, had never seen the viciousness we were now witnessing. The violence was overwhelming at times. Bodies were badly mangled from the arsenal of weapons being used on both sides. When Japanese sites were finally overrun, it was often difficult to identify which side a corpse belonged to, often being the leggings that the legs bore that made it possible . . . the Japanese being made of khaki and the Americans canvas. Limbs were everywhere, often fifty or more feet from the torso from which they had been detached.

"I've never seen anything like this before. We thought Tinian was bad, but I hope I never see the likes of this again."

"Lieutenant, I think you need to come over here."

"What is it, Sergeant?"

I walked to where the sergeant was pointing.

I looked at the mangled remains of a Marine lying next to a bunker, now silenced.

The sergeant handed me a set of dog tags.

I almost got sick when I saw the name.

"Jesus" was all I could mutter.

I read the name again.

David Peterman.

I turned to the sergeant.

"He was my roommate for a short time while we were recuperating on Maui. He was from Wisconsin. He shared his fears with me that he might not make it home . . . but I never dreamed it would have to be like this."

I turned my head away from the sergeant as tears began to well up in my eyes. As I stood thinking about our conversations, my thoughts were shattered by a sudden burst of gunfire that passed to my right side.

"Take cover men. Damn Nips. I thought we had those pillboxes and bunkers secured. How the hell do they keep reinforcing them?"

As the battle proceeded, it would become obvious that the tunnels that had been dug interconnected most of the island, allowing the Japs to replace gunners into bunkers that had been taken but then left unoccupied thinking that they had been rendered harmless.

"Get some flamethrowers up here. We're going to roast those bastards out of there."

A corporal came galloping up carrying the heavy pack on his back, called an M2-2, filled with gasoline mixed with a thickening agent called napalm. It used nitrogen as a propellant and the flammable mixture was ignited as it exited the barrel of the device. It could effectively deliver its deadly cargo several hundred feet and was a major psychological deterrent to its enemy. Practically, it was most effective cleaning out nests of the enemy after they had been rendered partially neutralized by gunfire or hand grenades.

"Corporal, I want you to be ready to torch that bunker just as soon as we can get some fire in there."

"Yes sir!"

I led two other members of the squad toward the objective, and using hand signals prompted them to fan out. They all moved in a crouching position until they had the bunker surrounded.

I signaled again: "On my mark".

After about thirty seconds I gave the signal and the three of them all converged on the opening. They initially threw grenades and then charged as soon as the explosions occurred, firing into the bunker interior.

"Now" I said to the corporal carrying the flamethrower.

Instantly he was there and dousing the bunker with the flaming liquid. In a flash, men were jumping through the opening, draped in flames and screaming in agony as other members of the squad shot them, putting them out of their misery. Once they were sure the bunker was clear, I climbed inside to inspect the area. I was surprised to find a door in the floor. We all stood carefully by as the sergeant raised the door held in place by hinges on one side.

"Well, I'll be damned."

There was a stairwell leading into the underground system of tunnels that we had heard so much about.

"Someone get a light over here" I yelled.

The corporal with the flamethrower detached a flashlight he had strapped to his utility belt. The stairs went down at least twenty feet before leveling out into the tunnel that presumably interconnected it with other parts of the island.

"No wonder they keep these things going even after we've cleaned them out. Sergeant, let's get some ordnance over here and see if we can't give them a little present."

We stuffed some backpacks with grenades and mortar rounds and lowered them into the tunnel. We had planted wire into the packs and as soon as they were in place, hooked the wire to the detonator device.

"All clear!

Fire in the hole!"

The sergeant rotated the handle setting off an explosion that no doubt was audible all the way to the water line. After the dust had settled, we inspected our handiwork. The opening had been completely sealed and hopefully some of the blast had done damage on the other side as well.

"O.K. men. Let's get to that quarry."

Chapter Twenty-Three

Meanwhile, at the base of Mt. Suribachi, weather continued to impede any progress that our Marines had hoped for. The rain turned the volcanic soil into a muddy glue, further hampering any attempts by the Sherman tanks to assist in the assault.

On D+4, the 28th Marines finally got a break thanks to improving weather. They prepared to scale Suribachi, expecting fierce resistance as they had previously encountered; but the Japanese were almost nowhere to be found as the Marines rose to the summit. Apparently the enemy was content to stay inside their tunnels and other fortifications within the mountain.

Later that afternoon, after the squad that had reached the summit sent word back to headquarters that they had taken command, another squad bearing an American flag and a makeshift flagpole raised it for all to see, inviting a photographer, Joe Rosenthal, to capture the moment. Even though the Marines had a long way to go before victory would be complete, the site of the flag on the peak of Suribachi was a great morale boost for everyone. The Japanese were quite aware that the Marines had advanced further than they had anticipated in such a short period of time.

Major Yonomata, a commander of Japanese forces on the island, summarized it well:

"Those of us who are left fully realize that our hopes of repelling the Americans or living to return to our homeland and loved ones are out of the question.

We are doomed."

Back to the east, the 27th regiment and several fellow regiments of the 4th and 5th Marines continued to press forward towards Airfield #2 and the northern sections of the island. Most days were marked by slow progress and then backtracking as the resistance increased. The medics were overwhelmed by the numbers of casualties the Marines were taking; the wounded often lay moaning in agony for hours before they could be transported back to the beaches and evacuated to hospital ships. Others died before anyone could even administer morphine and give them brief solace before they succumbed to their mortal wounds.

The dead and wounded were approximating over a thousand a day following the six thousand estimated killed or wounded on the first day alone. My squad had been reduced to a mere shadow of the group that had disembarked onto the island only days earlier.

The Seabees were already busy repairing and lengthening airfield #1, so that the B-29 superfortress bombers along with the P-51 Mustangs and P-61 night fighters would have a launching facility toward mainland Japan. And along the western coast near Mt. Suribachi, they were preparing facilities for the amphibious Catalina and Coronado flying boats.

But the fighting continued in earnest. The center of the island became the next major objective as the Marines began to surround the Japanese. The 9th Marines began the assault but soon realized the fury of their enemy. Despite being aided by more than twenty Sherman tanks, naval gunfire and air support, they were soon thrown back by a combination of machine gun fire, mortar rounds and anti-tank rounds. The enemy had the advantage of the height of a three hundred and sixty feet high rocky ridge named "Hill Peter". Together with elements of the 3rd and 5th divisions, they surrounded the western and northern sections. On the right flank, the 4th Marines encountered four formidable defensive positions that collectively became known as the "meatgrinder".

Hill 382 (named for its elevation above sea level) was the first of these laden with pillboxes, caves, dug-in tanks, enfiladed artillery positions and bunkers; it was followed by the "amphitheater" . . . a shallow depression some four hundred yards to the south; and just to the east of it a prominence called "Turkey Knob" on which sat a huge block house and observation post. Lastly, there was the village of Minami, partially destroyed by naval gunfire but still housing numerous gun emplacements. The Marines, not knowing what lay ahead attacked "Hill 382" but made little if any gains that first day as their Sherman tanks became bogged down in the wet volcanic ash.

And to the west, the 24th Marines (3rd Division) were slugging their way around Airfield #1, trying to clear the way for the Seabees to complete the repairs of the badly damaged runways for use by Allied Forces. Colonel Ikeda of the Japanese command anticipated their moves and had mines planted in strategic places, so that approaching tanks were disabled. This led to fierce hand to hand combat as the Marines encountered the enemy protected by bunkers and pill boxes. But by the end of day D+5, the area was secured, albeit at a high cost of lives on both sides.

"Sergeant, we've got to get off this hill. If we stay here much longer, there won't be any of our squad left."

My men and I had foraged to the top of 382, joined by members of the 24th. But after a day of fighting, no progress had been made and casualties continued at an appalling rate. The numbers of enemy fortifications and troops occupying the area signaled that this was to be their final line of defense. There would be no retreating from the "meatgrinder". With reinforcements from the 27th Marines, the battle continued into the next day when finally aided by rocket fire from multiple launcher trucks, we succeeded in taking it and moving on into the flats of the "Amphitheater" and toward "Turkey Knob".

The former had two prominences, "Hill Peter" and "Hill Oboe", both formidable and well protected as had been 382. Beleaguered by days of fighting and overwhelming numbers of casualties, the Marines launched a final push on the afternoon of D+8, taking first "Hill Peter" and then "Hill Oboe", finally securing the perimeter of Airfield #1 and allowing the Seabees *to finish their work without significant risk. My men and I took a short break before setting our sights on the next objective, the "Turkey Knob".*

"Lieutenant, how much longer do you think it's going to be before this Godforsaken island is secured?" I turned to address the question from the private who had been with me since we came ashore nine day earlier.

"Riley, I wish I knew the answer to that. The brass would have had us believe that this small piece of real estate would be ours in a matter of days. They assumed that with all the pre-invasion bombardment that resistance would be light. And on D-Day, that was also the initial impression . . . until we were well onto the beaches and all hell broke loose. Just keep your head down and do your job like you've been doing and everything will be just fine and soon we'll all be headed back to Maui. I'd like to think that it's just a matter of days now."

As I was finishing the sentence, the sound of enemy fire began again. I turned to look towards the origin of the fire. When I turned back toward Private Riley I almost broke into tears. Riley's body was crumpled on the ground with half his head blown off by a bullet that had whistled by a moment earlier.

"Son of a bitch.

We've got to stop these bastards once and for all."

I snatched the dog tags from around Riley's neck and motioned to my remaining men to move out. We were obviously sitting ducks where we were.

Like the ebb and flow of the tide, the battle raged and ground was gained and then was lost. By the end of another week, little had been accomplished, but the attrition rate continued to grow. My frustration . . . as well as that of my comrades . . . was growing daily. One giant final push against the enemy was what was needed so that we could wrap up the campaign and go home to Maui. Helen was in my thoughts constantly, but her image was becoming ethereal . . . it had been almost two years since I had seen or held her. Letters from her were undoubtedly being sent, but in the midst of battle, there was no mail delivery. I could only look forward to reading dozens of her warm missives upon my return to the Hawaiian Islands.

135

One Marine made a diary entry that was later published concerning the waiting game both sides were playing: "There is a quiet deadly stillness in the air, the tension is strong, everyone is waiting. Some will die—how many, no one knows. God knows, enough have died already."

On D+15, the time was ripe and the order to advance on the objective at all costs was given by General Schmidt. The enemy positions were pounded by Corsair and Dauntless aircraft, dropping bombs and napalm. This time elements of the three main divisions, the 3rd, 4th and 5th, all sent men forward and for the first time as they mounted a ridge they were able to see the ocean in the near distance.

But despite the aid of aircraft, tanks and ground support using flamethrowers, we were held some quarter mile from our beach objective by an increasingly desperate enemy who managed to continue resupplying bunkers and pillboxes with men and ammunition.

The 27th regiment, my own, had been decimated by the continuing vicious attacks being thrown at us.

The following morning, D+16, the signal was given at 0500 to commence the attack. My remaining men and I had radioed our location on a small perch called Hill 362C; unfortunately, the information was inaccurate since we were actually on Hill 331, some two hundred and fifty yards to the southeast.

"Men, we've got to make our way to the correct position or risk getting hit by our own artillery."

As we advanced through terrain where only light resistance had been reported, a Japanese soldier in one of the machine gun nests spotted us as we rounded the hill prominence and opened fire killing several of my men and almost hitting me in the process. At the same time, a single soldier fired from my right and I took him out with a single burst from my rifle.

"Sergeant!"

I reeled around to check behind me only to see the body of my first sergeant ripped to shreds by the burst from the machine gun. Several others also lay wounded and dying just beyond the sergeant.

"Jesus! That only leaves me and one private" I whispered to myself.

"Jones, help me get these wounded under cover of those bushes. Medic!"

There was no response coming.

The Navy corpsmen had had the ominous duty of trying to help the dead and dying amidst the steady stream of bullets and other ordnance . . .

and themselves had paid a terrible price along with their comrades from the Marines.

The entire sector was devoid of any fellow Marines and for the first time since D-day, I felt strangely alone. It was just me and the private. No experienced non-com to help lead the way as before. I briefly thought of Helen and all our plans, but I knew what I had to do.

"Jones, cover me. We've got to take out that machine gun or we'll never make it to Hill 362.

"But, Sir . . . ."

"Do as you're told Marine."

"Yes, Sir."

I crawled toward the bunker where the machine gun fire had originated. I approached from the gunner's blind side, slid to just below the opening and lobbed in two grenades simultaneously. As I slid back to safety, the grenades exploded sending shrapnel and smoke bellowing from the bunker. There was no sign of life, no screams to indicate anyone had survived the blast. I cautiously made my way back to the opening, shoved the barrel of my machine gun into the bunker and fired several bursts.

There was no answer.

I surveyed the bunker through the opening and saw that there had been only two Japanese soldiers manning it and both were dead. As I turned back toward Jones, I saw a wounded Jap soldier rise up from behind a large bush and aim at the private. I quickly dispatched him with a burst from my gun.

I worked my way back to my only remaining man.

"O.K. Private, let's get the hell out of here."

The private was still shaking from the thought of almost being killed.

"That was a mighty brave thing you did, sir."

"Well, Private, it's my job to protect you and our dead and wounded boys and to get us out of here alive." I tried my best to answer him with sincerity and humility. I knew how scared he was.

I rechecked my map and saw our position. Hill 362C lay just northwest of our current position and . . . I assumed . . . it was heavily fortified between the two.

"Private, we've got to get out of here and we must take the dead and wounded with us."

We crawled back to the bushes that covered the three men we had rescued earlier.

"*Taylor's dead. But we can't leave anyone here. The Japs are brutal to the dying and they love to mutilate corpses. We'll have to take turns moving them forward.*"

I took some branches from the bushes that had covered the men and lashed several together to make a pallet similar to a wiki up that I remembered seeing in the cowboy and Indian movies as a kid.

"*Help me with this, Jones. We'll have to stay low, take them one at a time for ten or twenty yards and then come back for the next one. You can stay at the forward position each time as we move and I'll shuttle them forward.*"

"*Yes, sir.*"

Stray bullets and mortar fire continued to whiz over our heads as we undertook the tedious task of moving from Hill 331 towards Hill 362C where we hoped we would rejoin members of the 4th and comrades from the other regiments that had been forced to band together as the numbers in our groups continued to dwindle. Moving ten to twenty yards at a time, Private Jones and I dragged the make shift wiki up with its cargo of dead and wounded Marines . . . although all succumbed before we were rescued. We had advanced almost fifty total yards when a sudden burst of machine gun fire from a bunker well concealed by foliage just ahead of us sprayed the area, wounding the private in his right arm.

I took a bandana from around my neck and used it to fashion a tourniquet around his arm. Judging from the amount of bleeding coming from the wound, it was apparent that some major blood vessel had been injured.

"*Sir, I don't think I can help you anymore*" he uttered just as he went into a slumber.

"*Damn. He's going into shock.*"

I quickly repositioned the private with his head down and rechecked the tightness of the tourniquet. It appeared to be controlling the bleeding. But if I was going to save the private, I would have to get some help. It was late afternoon, so I decided to wait until dark before proceeding to seek help. I knew if I attempted to yell for help it would signal our position to the enemy . . . if they were still in the nearby bunker. Some rounds had landed nearby the bunker during the time we had lain there, so I couldn't risk being detected.

The private was alive, but his pulse was weak and he remained unconscious. As I waited for the gathering darkness, I remembered Helen's face and thought of our times together and our dreams for the future.

"I won't let you down" I vowed.

"I'll come back to you just as I promised."

With that thought racing through my head, I checked my position and kept moving with hopes of finding my comrades.

Chapter Twenty-Four

I had completed at least five round trips, ferrying the dead and now Private Jones toward our objective when I collapsed in utter exhaustion. For most of the time, there was just random gunfire as I attempted to stay below the line of sight of the Japanese soldiers poised in the bunkers and pill boxes all along the ridge to my north.

"Lieutenant, come here and look at this!"

Elements of the 3rd division had been inching their way in the same direction, toward Hill 362C, adjacent to the small town of Nishi on the northwest coast of the island. Private Jones, who had been virtually comatose during the evacuation, opened his eyes at the sound of the sergeant's voice. He mumbled some words as the Lieutenant approached.

"What's he saying?" the lieutenant queried the sergeant.

"I'm not sure . . . something about the lieutenant dragging all of them here."

"Get our medic over here."

The Navy corpsman was there in an instant assessing the private's wound.

"Looks like he's got a major vessel injury. The tourniquet around the entrance wound has stopped the bleeding, but I'm not sure his arm is going to survive. It may need to be amputated. I'm going to try loosening it up."

As soon as he began to loosen it, blood immediately spurted from the injury site.

"No question, sir, it's an arterial injury. Otherwise, it should have stopped bleeding by now."

He reached into his medic's bag and retrieved a hemostat and some suture material.

"I'm going to try and put a stitch on it. Hopefully I can stop the bleeding, but it will also cut off the circulation to his forearm and hand like the tourniquet has been doing all this time. I doubt we can save the arm."

"Do what you have to do, doc" was all the lieutenant could add.

I had succumbed to the fatigue induced by my efforts to move my men out of harm's way. As the corpsman worked on Private Jones, I suddenly became aware of the voices and activity around me.

"Lieutenant, I see you're back with us. I'm 2nd Lieutenant Rod Turlington and this is Sergeant Sam Weems. We're with the 3rd division. We've been trying to reach that damn Hill 362C for days. I think we're finally going to make it.

Care to join us?" He smiled as he posed the rhetorical question to me.

I responded in kind.

"We would love to join you, Lieutenant. My men and I . . . we were caught in a crossfire between those damn bunkers just ahead and a few elements that came at us from the east. We managed to take them out, but I lost all of my men except Private Jones in the process."

He reached out to help me up from the ground.

Name's Mathews, lieutenant. Jim Mathews."

"How are you coming with that arm, doc?"

"I've got the artery controlled, sir, but it doesn't look good overall. Let me put a clean dressing on it and then we'll be ready to move out."

Lieutenant Turlington turned toward me.

"Sir, with your permission, I'll take the lead."

Extremely fatigued by the events of the past day, I nodded my approval.

Turning toward the corpsman and seeing the dressing now in place on the private's arm, the Lieutenant gave the order.

"Let's get the hell out of here.

I've got a hankering to see that damn ocean everyone keeps assuring me is just a short distance away."

❦

D+19 was the key day, for it was then that the Japanese forces were divided in two as the Marines made their way into the little coastal town of Nishi, thereby leaving the main pocket of resistance on the northern coast of Iwo Jima. General Kuribayashi had relocated his headquarters to the remote northern coastal fortresses, knowing that this would be the scene of the final defense of the island. While he never expected to return to his native Japan alive, he felt that he and his men had gallantly served their homeland by the delaying tactics and heavy casualties that they had inflicted on the United States.

General Schmidt knew that the final thrust would be costly as well since the Japanese code would not allow surrender at any cost. Two areas of concern, "Cushman's Pocket" and "The Gorge" still needed taking. The final push by Marines using flamethrowers, explosives and small arms was preceded by bombing and strafing by P-51's. Airfield #1 was now in use as a secondary landing site for damaged B-29's. Most of the Naval vessels had deployed to Guam in anticipation of the invasion of the Japanese mainland that was in the planning stages.

Elements of the 3rd, 4th and 5th Marines spent the next eight days "mopping up" with the loss of several thousand additional men as the Japanese soldiers remaining had to be literally dug out of their entrenchments rather than surrender. Admiral Nimitz's bulletin on March 17th, nine days before the official end of hostilities, that "the island was officially secured" had been unfortunately premature.

❦

"Captain Mathews, it seems you've had a rather exciting couple of days."

I looked up at the colonel addressing me. Still fatigued from the events that occurred while rescuing my men from the onslaught of Japanese troops fighting the futile final days of the assault on Iwo Jima, I didn't realize that I had been transported to a ship moored just off the west coast of the island.

"Yes, sir, I guess I have. But . . . captain?"

"Private Jones here tells us that you were single handedly responsible for saving his life and rescuing the bodies of at least a half dozen of your men and some from the other units that had joined you. And that you took out at least twenty-five Japanese soldiers in direct combat as well as a bunker when you crawled up to it and destroyed it with hand grenades. I want you to know that you have exceeded the standards for conduct in combat and that you're being recommended for the Medal of Honor.

And your C.O. has approved your immediate promotion to captain."

I was stunned.

"But, sir, I only did my duty . . . I only did what I've been trained to do . . . what any Marine would do given the same circumstances. I'm afraid the true heroes are the ones who fought out there beside me, who won't be going home to resume their lives with their families and loved ones. They gave their lives that I might have mine.

I'd like to rejoin my unit if I can, sir."

"Jim, the battle is over. Iwo is ours and you're heading back to Hawaii for some well deserved R & R . . . and then you're going home. The commandant has ordered that all Medal winners and candidates be sent back to the states right away to help in the war effort.

Captain, I'm proud to shake your hand and I wish you Godspeed."

Well, I didn't know what to say.

"Thank you, sir."

⤸

I would never forget a quotation I later heard attributed to an Iwo Jima Marine:

"When you go home, tell them of us and say: 'For their tomorrows, we gave our todays.'"

⤸

Maria stopped the VCR at her mother's request.

"No wonder it was so hard for him to talk about it over all these years. And I can see why he became so emotional every time anyone brought up the war, and every Memorial Day when we visited the cemeteries where veterans were buried.

And not wanting to visit the battle sites like so many other veterans of the Pacific war; I'm not sure I would have wanted to visit the islands where all this took place either. Seeing where his men died would have brought back much too vivid memories.

Let's continue."

CHAPTER TWENTY-FIVE

While the "mop up" of Iwo Jima continued for nine days following Admiral Nimitz's declaration that "the island is now secure", with the loss of several hundred Marines, thousands of injuries, and countless Japanese fatalities as they fought hand to hand at the northernmost part of the island, I was on my way back to Maui en route to the United States mainland. Elements of my regiment, the 27th, along with other members of the 3rd, 4th and 5th divisions finally secured the island on the 26th of March, nineteen forty-five. The final tally for American casualties exceeded twenty-three thousand with almost six thousand deaths. The Japanese death count was almost twenty thousand out of a garrison of slightly over twenty-one thousand. Approximately a thousand were taken prisoner and a few were never accounted for, including General Kuribayashi who was rumored to have led the final charge.

Private Jones and I were taken to Maui aboard a hospital ship. Unfortunately, Jones had to have his right arm amputated as gangrene had set in due to the injury to his major blood vessel and the contamination on the jungle infested island.

We arrived there about ten days later. Jones was quickly transferred to a faster ship and continued on to Pearl Harbor and the U.S. Naval

Hospital where he could receive maximum care. He was soon on his way to Washington where we would eventually be reunited.

⌘

"Sir, these are for you."

I looked up and smiled at the corporal performing mail call duty.

"Thank you" I said softly. I was resting at the field hospital on Maui while waiting to be transported to the states.

In my hand were two bundles of letters from Helen. I gently pressed my nose against the envelopes, taking in her scent. Then I organized them by post marks and began with the first and read all the way to the last which had been written only about two weeks earlier. Things at home were fine, reports that the war effort was going well instilled optimism in everyone, but news of the terrible fighting on Iwo Jima left her not knowing from day to day if she would be the next one to receive a dreaded telegram with news of my death or severe injury . . . or perhaps worse, notice of my being missing in action. I was lost in the reverie of her words and memories of our times together which now seemed an eternity ago, when my thoughts were interrupted by the same corporal that had brought the mail several hours earlier.

"Sir, the colonel says that you are welcome to use his secure telephone to call anyone you like back home. He also asked me to tell you that you're to be flown to Pearl Harbor in the morning and from there back to the states, to Washington, D.C.

He also would like to see you at your earliest convenience."

"Please tell the colonel that I will be there as soon as I put on my uniform."

"Yes, sir." The corporal gave me a crisp salute and scampered off to the colonel's office.

I had been lying in my trousers and t-shirt only. I put on my regulation blouse and tie and proceeded to the colonel's office. The sergeant in the outer office ushered me right in.

"The colonel asked to see me" I said to Colonel Withers.

"Jim, let me be the first to congratulate you. I just received word from the commandant's office. It's official, you're to receive the Medal of Honor."

The colonel gave me a crisp salute!

"It's my honor to have had you in my command if only briefly."

"Thank you, sir.

And now if you don't mind, sir, I'd like to take you up on that offer to place a call to the states."

The colonel smiled.

"Somehow I don't think you'll be calling your mother."

I didn't have the heart to tell him of mother's death while I was in combat. I just smiled in return and sat down with the phone as he exited the office and closed the door.

I had to think what day it was and what date and approximate time it would be in Washington, D.C. With the help of the joint overseas operator that I had been connected to, I now knew that it was late Sunday night in D.C. I gave the number of the boarding house to the operator and sat and listened as the call was forwarded through a series of relays, finally ending at the Marine Corps Commandants office that then rang Helen's residence.

After an eternity of rings, someone finally answered the phone.

"Yes, she's in her room. May I say who is calling?"

"It's a surprise! Tell her it's a long overdue call."

There was a lengthy pause on the other end.

"Please hold, sir. I'll get her for you."

Helen was asleep when she heard the knock on her door. The voice on the other side was quite animated. She opened the door quickly, not being sure what to expect at such an ungodly hour, for it was now after midnight.

"What is it Marie?"

"I think it's your fiancé!"

Helen stood there stunned for a moment.

"Jim.

My Jim?"

"I think so."

They both hurried down the steps to the parlor where the phone was located. Marie handed it to her.

"Jim, is that really you?"

"Hello, sweetheart.

Yes, it's really me. How are you?"

"Never mind me, how are you?

Where are you?"

"I'm fine and I'm back in the Hawaiian Islands. Iwo Jima turned out to be a little more of a problem than the folks in Washington counted on, but it's ours now and we're well on the way to winning back the Pacific.

Helen, I'm being sent back to Washington. I'm being flown to Honolulu tomorrow and then back to the states . . . ."

"Jim, you're not hurt are you?" Helen interrupted me in mid-sentence.

"Only a scratch or two. No, it's nothing like that.

For some strange reason, they're going to award me the Congressional Medal of Honor, so President Roosevelt has ordered me stateside. There'll be an award ceremony at the White House and then they want all the medal recipients to go on a trip around the country to bolster the war effort and encourage people to buy war bonds."

Helen didn't quite appreciate the significance of all that I had just said, but she clearly heard the part that I would be returning to Washington.

"When will you get back here? Oh, darling, I can't wait to see you and see that you're really all right."

"I don't know just yet. Just as soon as I get to Pearl Harbor and find out the schedule, I'll call you. You're all I've thought of Helen. You were with me every moment during the battles I fought in. You kept me going when things were not going well."

Helen could hear my voice crackling as I spoke.

She sobbed audibly.

"Oh, Jim. I love you so much. Hurry home to me."

"I'll try to call you sometime tomorrow or the next day at the latest.

I love you, too."

My finger pressed the receiver, ending the call. My eyes too were misty with emotion.

"Sir, are you finished?"

The operator had been instructed to monitor my call and make any others that I wished to place.

"Yes, thank you operator."

The following morning, an amphibious PBY made a special trip to Maui to ferry me, along with some wounded, back to Honolulu. We landed *at nearby Ford Island and then I was taken directly to an adjacent pier where a naval vessel was preparing to sail to San Diego.*

"Jim, I'm sorry we can't get you home a little quicker, but all aircraft are needed in theater; we'll have you back in California within seven to ten days depending on the weather. From there, I can assure you there will be a flight standing by to take you to Washington. The President wants to shake your hand and personally place that medal around your neck at a White House ceremony."

I thanked the lieutenant commander who had escorted me to the ship. I made my way up the gangplank, saluted the ship's fantail according to naval tradition, and asked permission to come aboard.

"Welcome aboard Captain Mathews. It's our pleasure to escort you home.

I'm Commander Walters, skipper of this vessel, and we'll try to make the crossing as smooth and fast as we can. I know you'd like to get home as soon as you can . . . wherever that may be."

"It just so happens that home for me is where my girl is, and that's Washington, D.C. And it just happens to be where the White House is located as well."

"An amazing coincidence" added the commander.

"Boats, show our special guest to his quarters, and then let's get underway."

"Aye, captain."

CHAPTER TWENTY-SIX

The weather was cooperative and the seas were relatively smooth the whole way from Hawaii to San Diego, the ship's home port. Exactly one week had elapsed since we set sail from Pearl Harbor. As promised, just as soon as I had set foot on land, I was greeted by a Navy chief who had been appointed my escort.

"Captain Mathews, Chief Joseph Abernathy at your service. I'm to escort you to the airfield where a flight is waiting to take you directly to Washington. President Roosevelt is expecting you and several other medal winners at the White House on April 14th. That should give you a few days to get yourself ready for the big event. Are you married, sir, or do you have someone awaiting your return?"

"As a matter of fact, someone is waiting and she'll need a little time to get ready for the White House ceremony. By the way, Chief, is there a telephone handy?

I promised her I'd call just as soon as I arrived in California and let her know when I'll be home."

"I'm sure they have one at base ops. Also, you can catch up with the pilots of your aircraft and get your schedule from them."

We proceeded to the chief's vehicle and left for the airfield at Coronado. The drive was short, only about ten minutes.

"Here we are, sir."

The chief escorted me into the operations tower and introduced me to the pilots who were anticipating my arrival.

"Captain, it will be our pleasure to escort you to Washington. I'm Lieutenant Charles Wilson and this is our co-pilot, Lieutenant Jake Smith."

We all shook hands.

"How soon will we be leaving and when do you expect us to arrive in D.C.?

"We're at your disposal, Captain. We'll need to stop three times en route to refuel so I would expect us to arrive in Washington at Andrews Field about eighteen hours after takeoff, weather permitting. At this time of year, weather fronts with thunderstorms are frequent. Our reports indicate no serious weather across the country at the moment, but that can change."

"I need to use a phone to call my fiancée. Otherwise, I'm ready to go."

Lieutenant Wilson turned to the chief.

"There's one in the lounge, Chief. Please show him the way. We'll be getting the craft ready to roll just as soon as you're done."

∽

I was disappointed when the individual answering the phone at the boarding house couldn't find Helen.

"She's not here and I don't think she was scheduled to work today. Can I leave her a message?"

"Tell her that I'm leaving California right now and expect to be in Washington about this time tomorrow. We'll be landing at Andrews Field, just east of town. Tell her I'll call her just as soon as we land. If she's not going to be there, ask her to leave a number where I can reach her."

"To whom am I speaking?"

"I'm sorry." I didn't recognize the voice I was speaking to and realized the opposite was also true.

"This is her fiancé, Jim Mathews."

"Ah.

Captain Mathews. Congratulations, sir. I'm George Watson. I'm new here but I've heard all about you and Iwo Jima. I'm looking forward to meeting you. I'll tell Helen that you called and give her the information as you requested."

"Thank you, George."

With that, I walked to the waiting aircraft.

Climbing into the cabin, I shouted to Lieutenant Wilson:

"Let's get the show on the road."

The pilot plotted an essentially straight course between origin and destination. We made stops for refueling in Denver, St. Louis and Columbus, Ohio and then dead-headed on to Washington. With the three hour time change and a little extra time loss in Columbus due to a passing rain storm, we arrived at Andrews Field almost exactly twenty-four hours after leaving California.

"Sir, as soon as we're on the ground, we'll taxi to the terminal where there should be transportation waiting for you that will take you anywhere you like."

"Thanks, Lieutenant."

I felt the wheels hit the runway and grabbed my bag preparatory to deplaning.

"You're not in a hurry, are you sir?"

I laughed.

"It's been over two years since I've seen my fiancé. Phone calls and letters are nice, but I want to hold her and take in her scent once more."

"I understand, sir.

I had a girl once that I thought I would marry, but she took off on me while I was gone.

You're lucky."

The plane taxied up to the terminal and cut its motors.

"Good luck, sir."

I hurried down the ladder and started for the terminal where I expected to be met by the driver of the vehicle sent to escort me.

"Jim.

Darling."

I was dumbfounded. Helen came running toward me and slammed her body into mine. She threw her arms around my neck and gave me a big, lingering kiss.

"Oh. You feel so good."

Then she stepped back to get a look at me.

"A bit thinner than I remember, but everything appears to be intact."

She grabbed me again and we stood holding one another.

"God, you smell so good and feel even better. Is that a new perfume you're wearing?"

"You like it?

I got it especially for you. It's called Chanel Number Five."

"It's wonderful. But then, anything on you would be wonderful. How the devil did you know when I'd arrive?"

Helen smiled.

"I have my sources.

Now, why don't we get out of here and go somewhere a little more private?"

Helen pointed to a sergeant in the distance.

"He's here to take us anywhere we want to go.

I have a room at the Willard Hotel reserved for us."

"Wow. That's kind of fancy isn't it?"

"The military arranged it. You'd better get used to it. They seem to think you're some kind of special Marine.

And you know what, I agree with them."

She turned her head up toward mine and gave me another kiss.

We fell into bed immediately after being shown our suite at the Willard . . . that is, after we finally convinced the bellman that we didn't need anything else and had tipped him appropriately.

"You can't imagine how this feels to me" I uttered as I held her tight after our lovemaking.

"All those days and nights in the hellholes they sent us to. All the while, I dreamed of this moment . . . holding you, making love to you."

Helen began to weep.

"What's the matter, darling?"

"Oh, Jim. I was so afraid that you wouldn't come back to me.

All the news about the Pacific was so bad for so long, especially Iwo Jima. The reports kept indicating that things weren't going well and that the casualty rate was the worst of the war . . . and I was afraid every day that you would be next."

I pulled her closer. I had shared those precise thoughts every moment I was on Iwo, but I didn't want to frighten her any more.

"I'm here now, and they can't separate us again."

I sat up on the bedside abruptly.

"What do you say we get something to eat, and then you've got to start worrying about what you'll be wearing to our little outing at the White House on Saturday?"

"Do I really have to go with you? I'm not sure I'd know what to say to the President of the United States? Besides, it's still three days away."

"Well, I don't either, but I want to be able to show you off to President Roosevelt and anyone else that might be there."

She blushed. Then she grabbed my shoulder and pulled me back down onto the bed.

"One more round and then I'll be glad to join you for dinner."

With a a sudden gleam in my eye, I answered her.

"Anything you say, dear."

CHAPTER TWENTY-SEVEN

Though it was a Thursday afternoon, we were out shopping for Helen's new dress for the White House soiree. She had been given the rest of the week off from work after informing her boss of the impending big event; he was thrilled for her. Like most Americans, he had never had the pleasure of meeting the president personally even though they all worked for a federal agency located in Washington, D.C.

The afternoon passed slowly for me as I watched Helen try on a succession of dresses. Even though I had indicated that I thought several of them were quite exquisite, she wasn't satisfied that she had found the "perfect" one. While Helen was in the dressing room trying on one more dress, I became curious about all the sudden unusual activity occurring in the department store. People were scurrying about conversing with seemingly everyone they came in contact with. I walked over to the store security officer to enquire what was going on.

"They just announced on the radio that President Roosevelt died about one o'clock down at the little White House in Georgia."

"My God" was all I could think to say.

I turned and went back to the dressing room area where Helen had just appeared in the latest frock. She could see a changed expression on my face.

"Is something the matter?"

"The President is dead."

"Oh, my. He's been looking awful tired lately . . . but dead? How did it happen?"

"They haven't released any details yet, but I guess this obviously means that our visit to the White House is off for now. Had you decided on any of those dresses?"

"I think it can wait."

"I guess you're right. I'd better check with Marine Headquarters about what they want me to do.

Can you find your way back to the Willard? I'll join you there later."

"I'll take a cab. You do what you need to do and we'll get together later."

I kissed her on the cheek.

"I'll see you in a little while."

I was welcomed at the headquarters building by Colonel Robert DeHut. It was obvious that the medal winner's names and pictures had been circulated to all locations of the corp.

"Captain Mathews, it's good to see you here, but you know it's a terrible time for the country. President Roosevelt has become a fixture in our lives here in Washington. There are many who didn't like the man, but he got us almost all the way through this bloody war, and most will miss him. It's a shame he didn't live to see it to its conclusion.

You're staying at the Willard, I presume?"

The colonel was well informed and obviously overwhelmed by the news. I could see the moisture in the corner of his eyes.

"Yes, sir."

Then why don't you just wait there until you hear from me. I'm sure that your presence with one of the honor guard detachments would be much appreciated. We don't have an exact schedule of events for the president's funeral yet . . . he died in Georgia I guess you know? There's word that there will be a funeral procession by train bringing his body back to the capitol.

I'll call as soon as I know something."

"Thank you, sir."

I returned to the street where I hailed a cab that took me to the Willard.

✑

The late President's body was taken by train from Georgia to Washington, D.C. accompanied by an honor guard of Army soldiers from nearby Fort Benning, Georgia. It arrived in Washington early on Saturday morning, April 14, 1945. Mrs. Roosevelt had decided on a simple ceremony at the White House later that afternoon, after which the casket was once again placed on a train for the trip to Hyde Park, New York, the traditional Roosevelt home along the Hudson River north of New York City. The President would be buried in the family cemetery on the estate.

Harry Truman, Roosevelt's vice-president, had assumed the presidency shortly after news of the president's death reached the White House.

As a Medal of Honor recipient, I was assigned to stand duty at the White House, representing the United States Marine Corps, during the time the body lay in state following its arrival from Georgia early Saturday morning until its departure after the funeral services at the White House later that same day.

"I'll be back as soon as I can, dear. They'll be broadcasting the event on radio so you'll know when it's over. Afterward, if it's not too late we can get dinner."

"You just take your time and do your duty, Marine. I'm so proud of you. I'll see you tonight."

We kissed and I departed along with several other medal recipients also staying at the Willard.

✑

When I returned, it was late and Helen was asleep in a chair. I gently nudged her as I kissed her on the cheek.

"What time is it?"

"Almost midnight. After the casket was loaded on the train, we had to wait until the train departed. There was some minor problem with the engine, so it was almost two hours late leaving. Then we had to go back to headquarters to return our ceremonial rifles and swords. I don't have to report back until Monday morning. Hopefully, they'll be able to tell us when the medal ceremony will be rescheduled and what our next assignment will be and where.

Are you hungry?"

"Well, I didn't really have a regular meal all day, hoping you would get back earlier."

"I checked on the way in. They have a grille that stays open until two a.m. So what do you say?"

"I say, let's get something to eat."

Not surprisingly, being in Washington, D.C. and with the events of the week bringing people into town from all over the world, the grille on the ground level of the hotel was almost full.

"What do you like on the menu?" I asked Helen.

"Well, I don't like their prices. Imagine, seventy-five cents for a hamburger. It's outrageous."

I just smiled and squeezed her hand.

"Don't worry about that. Everything is on the house for us. So, what will you have?"

She settled on an egg salad sandwich, some French Fries and a Coke.

I ordered a steak sandwich, fries and a beer.

"Boy, what I wouldn't have given for one of these on Iwo" I said as I took a healthy sip of beer that was served in a frosty mug.

"Ahhh!"

Helen smiled. She was glad to see me enjoying myself, trying to imagine the hell that I had been through during my time in the Pacific. When we had finished our sandwiches, the waitress asked if we would like dessert.

I checked the dessert menu.

"You know, I can't remember the last time I've had a piece of apple pie with ice cream on it."

I looked at Helen.

"How about it?"

"Make it two" she said to the waitress.

"I'd like chocolate ice cream with mine," I added.

Helen threw me a strange look.

"Just one of my little quirks that you'll have to get used to."

It was almost two a.m. when we finally strolled back to our room. It had been such a pleasant and leisurely evening for the both of us that we didn't want it to end.

"You know, it's about time we tied the knot. It's time you were Mrs. Mathews . . . you've had that engagement ring on your finger for an awfully long time."

"That's the most wonderful thing you've said to me since you got home."

"Why don't we just sneak away somewhere and get married by a Justice of the Peace . . . that is, unless you really want to have a big church wedding with your family and everyone present?"

She smiled at me and gazed into my eyes.

"I always thought that's what I'd want. But, after all this time waiting for you to return . . . and now that you're here and you're safe, all I really want is you. So, why don't we make those arrangements . . . ?"

CHAPTER TWENTY-EIGHT

I returned late Monday morning after a meeting with officials at Marine Headquarters concerning the medal ceremony at the White House.

"With everything going on with the war, and having just assumed the presidency, Mr. Truman and his staff asked that it be delayed for about ten days and the commandant agreed. So, I have ten days off. Do you think that there is anything you might like to do during that time?"

Helen smiled coyly at me.

"Did you have something planned that you wanted to tell me about?"

"It just so happens that I have a friend in Quantico, Virginia . . . just thirty-five miles south of town. He and his wife would be thrilled to be witnesses at our wedding."

She grabbed my hand and started to cry. I pulled her close to me.

"I'll take that as a 'yes'. I'll call him later and make the arrangements. Perhaps you'd like to go shopping and buy that dress that you didn't get last week. Is it possible that you can wear it for our wedding and again to the White House?"

"That just might be possible."

"Typical vague response coming from a woman," I thought to myself. But I just let it pass.

"On second thought, I think I'll go call my friend now, before we go shopping."

In the lobby, I found a vacant phone booth and closed the door.

⌒∽⌒

The trip to Quantico took just a little over an hour in a car I borrowed from a fellow Marine medal winner.

"Helen, this is John Moffett and his wife, Marie. John and I served together at Camp Pendleton. He was the Ops officer."

"Helen, it's a pleasure to finally meet you" John offered. He leaned in and gave her a light hug.

"And this is Marie. We've been married for just over a year."

The women hugged each other.

"I've heard so much about you Helen. I'm so glad to finally make your acquaintance. And Jim, you must tell me some stories about your time together with my John. I'd like to know if some of the exploits you two had together are really true."

I smiled.

"We'll have to see about that later . . . but they probably are!"

Helen took a long hard second look at Marie.

"Can I assume you are in a family way?"

Marie turned with a stunned look on her face.

"Why yes. How did you know? I just found out myself about a week ago."

"Lots of pregnant women where I come from. There's just a certain look. So when are you due?"

"It will be sometime in January next year. But enough about me. Jim. Any news?"

"I contacted the local Catholic chaplain at the base before leaving Washington and he has agreed to officiate at our wedding. And he has agreed to a dispensation and will perform it any day of the week we choose given the circumstances. So we've picked tomorrow if that fits your schedule?"

John answered without hesitation.

"We're at your disposal."

"We're so glad to be able to help a fellow Marine, especially such a famous one" added Marie.

That kind of talk still made me blush.

161

"Please, I was just doing my duty.

Anyway, enough of that, how about dinner, my treat? Do you know any good places around here?"

"I think we can probably find a decent watering hole that also serves up a good steak."

"Lead on."

✑

Mike's Steakhouse was just what I had envisioned. All the popular brands of American beer, peanuts from a barrel that you ate and threw the hulls on the floor, and the best New York strip steaks that Helen and I had had in years.

John and Marie turned out to be very special people. Helen took to them right away, something she generally doesn't do until she has spent a good deal of time with someone. John and I had spent some extraordinary times together in the corps. Helen was beginning to learn about the special relationship that military men have with one other. I had mentioned many times about the camaraderie that developed among men whose lives depended upon one another in training and in actual combat . . . and it was on full display as we ate, drank and talked.

It was almost two a.m. when we finally returned to John and Marie's home. The couple had graciously insisted that we stay with them . . . after all, they were to be witnesses at our wedding the following day.

"I guess we'd better get some sleep. We need to be at the church at noon, and that's only a little over nine hours away."

We all said goodnight and went to our respective rooms.

"Today, I make you my wife" I said to Helen as I held her in my arms. "Finally, we legitimize our relationship."

"I've enjoyed being your woman regardless of the status you choose to confer on it."

She kissed me softly on the lips.

"Now, let's get some sleep. You'll want me to look my best for the wedding."

✑

"Father, this is my fiancée, Helen and these are our friends John and Marie Moffett who have agreed to be witnesses."

Father Daniel J. Burke had a heavy Irish brogue and hailed from the old school of priests. He had been ordained in County Cork in the old country and everyone couldn't help but know that fact since he repeated it often.

He shook everyone's hands.

"So, if everyone is ready, let us all proceed into the church. I arranged for our organist to provide a little music."

Helen and Marie waited in the vestibule while John and I walked briskly to the altar. Father Burke disappeared briefly into the room just off the main altar and reappeared dressed in his priestly vestments. He stood at the center of the altar, with John and I opposite the railing as the organist began with strains of "The Wedding March" by Mendelssohn.

Helen carefully walked the length of the church until she was abreast of me. Neither of us could conceal our joy at the occasion that we had anticipated for so long and thought might never come. We turned toward one another and held hands as Father Burke began.

"Dearly beloved, we are gathered here today to unite this man and this woman in the sacrament of Holy Matrimony. If anyone here knows any reason why these two should not be joined together, speak now or forever hold his peace."

We smiled and squeezed each other's hand. The vows were exchanged and the rings placed, and before either of us realized the service was almost at an end, Father Burke spoke one last time.

"By the power invested in me by the Holy Mother Church, and the state of Virginia, I now pronounce you man and wife.

You may kiss your bride."

I gathered Helen gently to myself and together we shared a kiss. As we stood savoring the moment, John and Marie interrupted us with heartfelt congratulations.

Father Burke shook my hand and accepted a small stipend for his troubles.

"Now you two be careful on your honeymoon and don't ever let me hear that anything has gone wrong with your lives together. You obviously were meant for each other. The Good Lord brought you back to take care of this woman" he said to me.

"Thank you, Father" we all added as we slowly walked to the door at the rear of the church.

Helen and I thanked the couple for their hospitality and got into our car that was waiting by the curb immediately in front of the church.

"We'll see you two in three or four days on our way back to Washington."

I helped Helen get situated in the car and glided out into traffic en route to a small cottage on the Virginia coast near Norfolk.

∾

"Well, we finally did it. Now, how about a little champagne?"

We had been told about this cottage sitting on a strip of land that fronted onto the Chesapeake Bay between Cape Henry lighthouse and a U.S. Naval instillation called Little Creek, where amphibious training was held preparatory to deploying to combat zones.

"Not that I deserve the medal" I said referring to the Congressional Medal of Honor, "but there certainly are some perks to it. The Commandant himself has stayed here in the past."

The cottage was actually an old home that had belonged to a former admiral's family and had been designated for use by high ranking Navy and Marine Corps officers and special guests, I of course falling into the latter category.

It generally was staffed by three or four enlisted Navy or Marine Corps personnel. But, considering that we were celebrating our honeymoon, we preferred to be completely alone. We spent the next several days getting reacquainted, taking walks on the beach, swimming and of course making love.

"I'm so glad your home . . . and safe. All those stories in the papers and on the radio about the battles in the Pacific . . . I was so scared. And there were so many people at work that got those dreaded telegrams from the War Department . . . I felt so bad every time I heard about one and wondered like everyone else if I would be next."

I pulled Helen closer.

"Well, my darling, now I'm here and you needn't worry anymore. I'm not going anywhere dangerous. And wherever they send me on their war effort program, you'll be right by my side."

"Jim, do you think they'll let me go with you?"

"I'll demand it. After all, I've got clout now. Besides, why wouldn't they want me seen with a beautiful woman?"

She leaned up and kissed me.

"You always know just what to say to make a girl feel special.

What do you say we call it a day and go to bed?" she added with a special twinkle in her eye.

"I'm right behind you" I answered as I turned off the lights in the den and followed her into the bedroom.

✧

The following morning we returned to Washington after a brief stop in Quantico to say hello to John and Marie and thank them again for their hospitality. Then I reported in to get the details about the presidential reception and the war bond tour.

"President Truman has requested our presence at the White House Tuesday night for the official Medal presentation."

"Would you mind terribly if I got another new dress? I think I'll preserve my wedding dress in case we have a daughter. She might like to wear it."

"My dear, anything you want to do is fine with me.

Then they're going to send us on a cross country tour along with some entertainers to bolster the war effort. They need our help selling War Bonds and getting people to enlist. The news coming out of Europe and the Pacific is good, but they don't want to let the effort lag. They need all the help they can get to sustain the final push.

And you're officially invited!"

"Jim, that sounds wonderful. Now, we'd better get going in case that dress needs any alterations.

Oh, I've so much to do."

Chapter Twenty-Nine

Tuesday, May 1, 1945 was a truly momentous day for us. Upon arriving at the White House by limousine, provided courtesy of the War Department to each of the Medal of Honor recipients, we were immediately ushered to the upstairs private residence where we were introduced to the President.

Harry Truman was a short, compact man who spoke with a middle American accent. His manner was friendly, his words personal. He invited us to sit down with him for a few moments.

"Jim . . . may I call you that Captain? . . . Jim your country and I are proud of you and all your comrades for the job you did in the Pacific, especially on Iwo Jima.

Helen, I'm sure you must be equally proud of your husband's accomplishments?"

"I am, Mr. President." Helen didn't think she should voluntarily add anything to her answer unless asked.

"Jim, I was a Captain in the artillery in the first World War, so I know something of what you must have gone through. I understand that those Japs were mighty tough, but we've got them on the run now."

"Yes sir, Mr. President" was all I could mutter. It's quite intimidating sitting next to the Commander-in-Chief.

The President asked us a few personal questions about our states of origin and then indicated that he would be seeing us at the presentation. We thanked him for his kindness and then we were escorted back downstairs to the main ballroom where dinner and the medal ceremony would be held.

"That went well, don't you think?" I whispered to Helen.

"I've never been in the presence of a President of the United States before . . . so I guess it did.

He's actually pretty personal, much like I had heard."

"He is. I'm favorably impressed."

"Jim!" said a voice from the corner of the room.

We both turned toward the voice.

It was another medal recipient that I had met several weeks earlier prior to the original planned event before President Roosevelt's death.

"Helen, this is Lieutenant Anthony Armstrong. He's another medal honoree.

Tony, this is my wife, Helen."

"I didn't think you were married?"

"That was two weeks ago. We were married just about a week ago. In fact we just got back in town a few days ago after a brief honeymoon on the Virginia shore."

"Well, congratulations to you both. I see they're signaling us to find our seats, so I hope to see you later."

We were seated at a table with several high ranking officers representing the United States Marine Corps and the United States Navy.

The President was announced and all stood as he and his entourage entered to strains of "Hail to the Chief". This was followed by a brief rendition of all the various service branch hymns.

Following benediction by the Chaplain of the Senate, dinner was served and all turned their attention to the delicious multi-course meal.

"Honorees, ladies and gentlemen, distinguished guests" . . . so began remarks by President Truman.

"I am humbled to be here this evening. As you all know, it was to be President Roosevelt's privilege to present these brave soldiers, sailors and Marines with our country's highest honor, the Congressional Medal of Honor.

We shall all miss his unmitigated enthusiasm towards our military. He had expressed to me on many occasions his admiration of the courage of our men and women in uniform, especially in times of war. While he never had the privilege of serving in combat as I did, albeit briefly, he felt a bond with those of us who did. His handicap kept him from serving, but not from rejoicing in the victories that you and your comrades have won for our country by your noble service.

I will not bore you with my own personal stories tonight, but rather ask Admiral William D. Leahy, my Chief of Staff for the military services, to assist me in the presentations."

With those brief words, Admiral Leahy joined the President on the dais and called forward the recipients individually and placed the medals around each of our necks. After we were all standing with the Admiral and President Truman, the entire audience stood and gave us a round of applause.

Helen was in tears, as were most of the people in the room at the sight of the brave men being honored. Two of the men had lost limbs, and one had been blinded in an explosion. She was thankful that I had returned intact and that we could face married life together without the handicaps that faced those injured honorees.

When the festivities had finished, and photos of the medal recipients alongside their Commander in Chief had been taken, we returned to our spouses or fiancées.

"You looked mighty handsome up there."

I turned toward Helen with tears in my eyes.

"I wish my entire outfit could have been here to accept this award. They deserve it far more than me."

Helen took my hand and held it in silence. It was not the first time I had reminisced like this . . . nor would it be the last. When the festivities had concluded, I asked if we could just go straight home. It had been an exciting day, but extremely taxing emotionally.

"Of course, dear" was all Helen could answer.

"It was a great evening, but all I could think about were the buddies of mine who didn't make it back from Saipan, and Tinian . . . but especially Iwo Jima. My God, they're the ones who should have been the guests of honor tonight . . . or at least their families. You and I have the rest of our lives *together, and what do they have? A loved one buried in some far off island cemetery that they'll most likely never have the opportunity to see . . . and memories of the past with no future like ours.*

It's just not fair."

Helen could see the emotion welling up in my eyes and remained silent, allowing me to reminisce.

Finally, I turned and motioned for her to join me.

"I'm so lucky to have you and to be here instead of still fighting in the Pacific on some Godforsaken island with a funny name. But if they'd let me, I'd go back . . . I owe it to my buddies who will be there forever."

Helen rested her head on my shoulder and again said nothing. She knew I was right about my feelings but she didn't want to encourage me to volunteer for additional war duty. I had done my job and my reward for it was to be here in the states in the service of my President, furthering the war effort by promoting War Bond sales.

When she lifted her head from my shoulder, she saw that I had drifted off to sleep.

She nudged me over onto the bed and put a blanket over me.

"Sleep well, my darling.

You've earned a good rest."

When I awoke the following morning, I chose not to mention anything about the night before.

"After breakfast, I'm heading down to headquarters to see if they have my orders all set."

Again, Helen didn't make any direct comments to me about my plans.

"Finish your eggs and bacon, dear. Would you like some more coffee with that?"

"No. I'm fine."

I finished breakfast and kissed her.

"I'll be back in a few hours."

When I returned early that afternoon, I was pretty much my old self again.

"I'm sorry about last night and this morning" I said as I kissed Helen as we stood in the doorway to our room.

She smiled.

"I understand . . . as best someone can who has never been there when you lost a best friend or comrade in arms."

I pulled her close and led her into the room and closed the door.

"Well, Mrs. Mathews, are you ready to take that tour of the United States with me? The War Department tour will take us from Boston and New York all the way to San Francisco and San Diego and back. We'll be on a special train, so there will be lots of stops. And, they promised each of us a room of our own on the train, meaning we can bring wives if we're married. And all meals and amenities will be provided as well.

I'm sure they'll have different types of festivities at each stop, too."

"Well, if you're sure that it's all right with your higher-ups . . . I'd love to go. You know my place is with you, Jim."

"Oh, I love you so much. Now, we leave tomorrow. First stop is Boston followed by several engagements en route back to New York City and Philadelphia; then we start the trek west, heading to Chicago with many small town stops in between."

"That sounds so exciting . . . getting to see all those places I've only heard about. And I get to do them all with you by my side."

"Now, I want to be fair . . . ."

Helen turned toward me expecting something untoward to come out of my mouth.

I raised a finger to her lips.

"I was just going to say that there may be times when I have to do things without you, meaning you may have to stay in our room on the train or in some lonely hotel room by yourself."

"Oh. I think I can find something to amuse myself with while you're gone. The important thing is that we'll be together."

I grabbed her and squeezed her tight, lifted her up and spun her around. Then we landed on the bed.

"Careful, you don't want to break it."

"No. But I would like to give it a little workout.

What do you say?"

"Well . . ." she uttered as she began to undress me.

CHAPTER THIRTY

Boston was experiencing a cool, wet spring, but the weather didn't dampen the spirits of the people there to greet the War Bond Victory Train as it came to be called.

We went from there to Springfield, Hartford, Albany and Syracuse before finally arriving in New York City on the evening of May 7, 1945.

The following day had been declared "Heroes Day" by proclamation of the city's then mayor, Fiorello LaGuardia. He and numerous other dignitaries were present to greet the medal winners at the newly occupied governor's home, Gracie Mansion.

It turned out to be an exceptionally auspicious day, since shortly after the welcoming ceremonies had begun, the mayor was handed a note by one of his staff. LaGuardia turned excitedly to the audience assembled.

"Ladies and Gentlemen, I have just been handed a note that contains the best news that I have heard in four long years.

The President of Germany, Karl Donitz, has just unconditionally surrendered all German forces to the Allies. It has also been reported that Adolph Hitler committed suicide about a week ago.

The war in Europe is over!"

There was near pandemonium as everyone in the crowd and on the dais looked for someone to hug or kiss or just find a hand to shake. I turned to Helen who was seated next to me and gave her a big hug and a kiss.

"Thank God, the killing in Europe will be over. Now, we need to quell the Japanese and end the war in the Pacific."

She squeezed my hand.

"Let us all stand and say a prayer of thanks" the Mayor continued after the audience had quieted down.

"And lest we forget what we came here for today . . . ." The Mayor introduced the guests of honor and encouraged everyone to continue to support the war effort since it was ongoing in the Pacific.

That night the largest celebration of VE day in the country was held in New York's Times Square and we were there amidst the revelers.

∞

"I can't believe that we're here together to celebrate such a glorious event. I always imagined that I would be sitting in a foxhole on some lonely Pacific island when the news came that the war was over . . . when our leaders finally came to their senses.

Well, at least Hitler is dead.

Now it's Japan's turn. And I should still be there with my buddies . . . if any of them are still alive."

Helen knew that I was hurting inside, that I felt that I hadn't done enough and that I still thought that taking me away from the action in the Pacific was just a form of abandonment.

"Let's try and enjoy the good news. Tomorrow is another day and you're doing your part to help win the war even if it's not with a gun."

I turned and looked longingly at Helen.

"Perhaps you're right. What do you say we go back to the hotel for a nightcap and perhaps a little one on one time?"

∞

"I still don't know how I got so lucky and found you. A man needs a woman like you . . . loving and caring."

"And a woman needs a man like you . . . loving and caring but also strong and principled. You make me so proud to carry your name. Growing

up, I always assumed I'd marry someone Italian like me. After all, almost everyone around me was from Italy or had Italian heritage. But thanks to getting ill, going to business school instead of finishing regular high school, and moving to Washington with the mayor . . . well, it's funny how life turns on a dime as the saying goes."

"And my getting sent there just at the right time and meeting you the way I did.

Here's to kismet."

Seated in a small bar just off the main lobby of the hotel with drinks in hand, I proposed a toast. The noise from outside was deafening even in the bar at the late hour just past midnight.

"There's talk now of an invasion of the Japanese mainland if the emperor won't surrender. I hope something happens to intervene in the event he doesn't. The loss of additional life would be horrendous."

I was getting morose again so Helen suggested we go upstairs to our room.

"I think I can suggest something to take your mind off of war."

One glance from her was all it took to change my mood.

The following day we boarded our train and headed west. Many stops were just to wave at the crowds gathered along the tracks or at a small station in some remote location. Generally, at least one of the medal winners said a few words of encouragement about the war progress to the people assembled, and asked them to support the War Bond effort. Often, the train would make twenty or more such stops in a single day before arriving at a major destination where we would disembark from the train and enjoy the luxury of a hotel room for the night.

"You look exhausted." I pulled Helen to my chest.

"I must say that all this traveling is a lot more tiring than I would have expected. I don't know how you and your fellow soldiers had the stamina to fight after traveling long distances in cramped ships.

Especially if you got seasick."

"I was lucky. I got a little nauseated a few times when the weather really roughened the seas. But some of the guys were miserable all the time. They spent most of the voyage hanging over the sides of the ship. They rarely could keep a meal down. I felt sorry for them as we were approaching our objective."

"Let's get to our room and freshen up and then we can get some dinner. At least we don't have any speaking engagements tonight."

༼

"Say, where are we anyway?"

Helen leaned over to look at the alarm clock on the bedside table. It was barely seven o'clock in the morning.

The days had blended into one gigantic blur. We had passed Chicago several days earlier and were heading for the west coast. We had made so many stops that she had honestly lost count of the number and locations.

I leaned over and opened the curtain on the window.

"Sign says North Platte, Nebraska."

"Oh.

Oh! I've read about this place. It's famous for the local ladies who make sandwiches and cookies for the troop trains passing through. They're known for entertaining them as well with dancing or just personal conversation. Lots of the boys heading for combat were welcomed here. For some, it was the last real personal human contact apart from their comrades that they had before meeting their fate on some Pacific island."

"You know, now that you mention it, I remember several guys in my outfit talking about some small town in the Midwest where they had stopped and were given such a warm welcome.

This must have been the place."

"Will we be here long?"

I had a copy of our itinerary on the table.

"It says we're having breakfast here and then continuing on towards Denver, Salt Lake City and Portland, Oregon with a bunch of quick stops between the last two."

There was a quick knock on the door.

"Breakfast in one hour inside the train station, Captain."

I acknowledged the porters message.

"Guess we'd better get dressed. I hear the food is really good. We wouldn't want to miss this now would we?"

༼

Several hours later, back on the train and once again headed west, we were talking.

"I have to say that the ladies there in North Platte are every bit as friendly as I had been told. It's a wonderful thing they have been doing all these years for our troops heading into harm's way. And I should congratulate them on their cooking. I don't know when I've had a breakfast like that . . . not even at home. The biscuits were wonderful and the breakfast meats must all be homemade too. I've never seen pork sausages so big and so tasty."

She glanced at me as I appeared to be dreaming.

"Sitting in the midst of combat on a desert island in the middle of the Pacific I never would have imagined any of this happening to me and you. I only wish we could send some of it to the ones still there."

Helen nuzzled her head against my chest. She knew that I was still hurting from the memories of my time there and of the men under my command that I had lost and of friends who didn't return alive.

She said nothing and let me reminisce.

From western Nebraska, the train dipped southwest to Denver and then on to Salt Lake City. Then it was on to Portland, Oregon where we had a two day stopover to give everyone on board the chance to rest, have a decent place to bathe and get a good meal.

"You're looking increasingly tired, darling" *I remarked to Helen as she came out of the bathroom after her shower.*

"Maybe I should have left you back in Washington. This has really been a grueling trip and there's a long way to go until we get back home."

She just smiled at me.

"And how would a girl get pregnant sitting at home all alone?"

I had all I could do to keep from falling over.

"Does this mean you're going to have a baby? I mean, are we going to be parents?"

"Yes to both questions" *she answered.*

"You know I thought maybe you were putting on a little weight around your hips . . . and your breasts are a little fuller . . . but I didn't want to *say anything. I thought it was probably due to all the good food they've been feeding us at all these small town stops and from all the sitting we've been doing in between.*

Oh, darling, that's the most wonderful news that I've had in an awful long time."

"Then you approve?"

Well, I took her into my arms and hugged her tightly, then quickly released her and stepped back.

"Oh, I guess I'd better be careful now that you're in that condition."

"That's all right, I won't break . . . at least not now."

Suddenly a thought hit me.

"But how can you be sure . . . that you're pregnant?"

She gave me one of those looks that only a woman can give her man.

"A woman just knows these things. As soon as we get home, I'll see a doctor."

"We have a weeklong stop planned in San Francisco. Maybe we can arrange for someone to see you there. After all, there are a number of military bases and medical facilities in the bay area."

"Perhaps. I guess maybe I should be taking some vitamins or something. O.K.

You can arrange it when we get there. I suppose that would be a good idea."

"Say, is there any reason we can't still enjoy each other?" I said leading her over to the bed and removing the towel that she wore after her shower.

"I can't think of a reason, can you?"

With that, I turned out the lights and slipped out of my clothes.

Chapter Thirty-One

We found the dispensary at Treasure Island Naval Station and stopped in hoping to find a doctor who could see Helen without an appointment. I went to the desk and showed my I.D. that contained a special affixed stamp identifying me as a medal recipient. The corpsman on duty excused himself and went in search of the physician in charge.

"I'm Dr. Hugh Wilson, Captain Mathews. It's my distinct honor to meet you. What can I do for you and your wife today?"

I turned toward Helen.

"My wife thinks . . . no, my wife is sure that she is pregnant. We were hoping someone could confirm that and then advise us about any medications she should be taking. We're on this War Bond selling tour and won't get back to D.C for another month or six weeks."

"Let me make a quick phone call, Captain."

Dr. Wilson returned about five minutes later with a Navy Commander in tow.

"This is our Chief of Obstetrics, Dr. Sam Maynard. He would be pleased to examine your wife and give us his official opinion and recommendations."

I turned to Helen who nodded, agreeing to go with Dr. Maynard.

"If you will excuse us, we'll be back shortly."

He led Helen down the hallway.

"If you would like some coffee, Captain, we have a fresh pot in my office?"

"That would be great. We got out kind of early this morning and didn't have time for breakfast."

We sat in Dr. Wilson's office chatting and sipping coffee for about thirty minutes until Helen reappeared accompanied by Dr. Maynard.

"Congratulations, Captain. I can confirm that your wife is indeed pregnant and already about eight weeks along. I've given her some instructions along with some prenatal vitamins that she should be taking. I would suggest that she see someone in D.C. just as soon as you arrive back there."

I looked at Helen, grinned and then gave her a big hug.

"So, we're really going to have a baby?"

"It appears so."

We stared into each others' eyes for a moment and then turned to our hosts.

"Dr. Wilson, Dr. Maynard . . . thank you both for your kindness, especially on such short notice."

"No, thank you for your service to our country, Captain" they both said almost in unison.

❧

Once outside the dispensary, I turned to Helen.

"I think we should go into downtown San Francisco and celebrate. We've got two days before we have to get back on that darn train.

What do you say?"

"Lead the way."

❧

We found our way to Fisherman's Wharf, a place we had heard about but somehow never imagined seeing, especially not under such wonderful circumstances . . . the Medal Tour and now news of Helen being pregnant with our first child.

"Oh Jim, it's wonderful here, although I'm a little cold. I always thought California was supposed to be warm and sunny year round."

"*I remember someone mentioning that San Francisco was a little different from southern California, that it gets cool ocean breezes even in the middle of summer. And fog . . . lots of fog that keeps temperatures down as well.*

Look over there at the Golden Gate Bridge . . . you can see the fog creeping in towards the bay."

She strained to look.

"*It's very wispy. I think I see a ship coming in.*"

Just then a horn blew indicating that indeed a ship was about to approach and pass under the bridge. We stood watching as it appeared to materialize out of nothingness.

"*Say, how about some seafood? I hear they have some of the best in the country. One of the guys at the hospital recommended we try Scoma's. It's supposed to be somewhere along here right on the water.*"

We walked a short distance and found a sign pointing the way to the restaurant that sat on a pier behind several other large buildings.

I approached the hostess and requested a table with a water view.

"*It'll be just a few minutes, sir. We've been very busy today, but considering your special occasion, I'll see what I can do.*"

I had confided Helen's delicate condition to the hostess. Momentarily, she returned and ushered us to a table overlooking the water with a spectacular view of the bridge.

Once seated, I turned and looked at Helen.

"*My darling wife, thank you for the greatest gift of all . . . a child.*"

I leaned across the table and kissed her softly on the lips.

She smiled in return.

"*Now, how about something to eat?*

After all, I'm eating for two!"

Two days later we were back on board the train headed toward Southern California with stops in Los Angeles and San Diego. Then the trek eastward along the southern route took us to Phoenix, Albuquerque, Dallas, Houston, New Orleans and finally Atlanta.

From there, it was back up the East coast and eventually Washington, D.C. As the train pulled into Union Station, Helen let out a sigh of relief.

"*You look tired, dear.*"

"It's been an exhausting trip, and the nausea was taxing. Thank God it seems to have let up now that I'm past the first three months."

As we stepped from the train, a familiar face was there to greet us.

"My God" yelled Helen.

"Look Jim, it's Betty Champagne."

The ladies screamed as they approached one another and hugged.

"Let me look at you" Betty said as she stepped back from Helen.

"When did you get pregnant? For that matter, when did you two get married?"

Helen recounted all the things that had occurred since they had last seen each other.

"And what about you? Did you and . . . Bob, wasn't it? What ever happened there?"

"Nothing. But . . . ." She held out her hand to show Helen a big diamond on her left ring finger.

"Well. Who's the lucky guy?"

"His name is Aaron Davis. He works for the Navy Department as a civilian contractor in their legal department. He was in law school when the war broke out, so they use him there with his knowledge of the law. He'll finish school when the war is over.

When I heard the train was coming back to D.C., I just had to see you two. I'd like to know if you would consider being one of my bridesmaids?"

Helen patted her stomach.

"I guess it all depends on timing. When are you planning on getting married?"

"Probably not until at least next year. It looks like the war could be over any time. Aaron has just one year left. So hopefully next summer."

"Then I'd love to be in your wedding."

I had remained quiet while the ladies talked.

"Betty, it's been great seeing you again, but Helen and I have to get going. I have to finish up some things from the tour at Marine Corps Headquarters and we need to get Helen to our hotel so that she can get some rest. It's been a long and grueling trip."

The ladies hugged once again. Betty promised to contact Helen with firm plans once they were made.

"What a nice surprise" Helen whispered to me as we stepped into the waiting car that would take us to the hotel.

"Yes" I agreed.

"*Now, let's get you situated and then I'll go finish my reports at headquarters.*"

⁂

It was early August and still the war raged on in the Pacific. I was hoping not to have to go back on the bond tour, and would have preferred a return to my outfit still in Hawaii . . . except for the fact that Helen was progressing with the pregnancy and I didn't want to miss being with her for the big event.

Early on the morning of the sixth, I was up fixing breakfast for Helen when I turned on the radio.

"*This is H.V. Kaltenborn, live on NBC News, bringing you a special report.*

We have just received word that the United States has dropped an atomic bomb on the Japanese city of Hiroshima. Reports are sketchy at this time but this is apparently a major industrial city in southwestern Japan on the main island of Honshu. Preliminary reports suggest that as many as fifty thousand or more people have been killed.

Stay tuned for more on this story as it becomes available."

I turned to walk back to the bedroom to tell Helen the news when I found she was standing behind me listening.

"*What exactly is an atomic bomb?*" *she asked.*

"*I'm not sure exactly, but word has been going around for some time that we were developing something that would make all conventional weapons obsolete.*

I guess maybe this is it."

"*So you knew about this?*"

"*Just rumors. It's all classified. I couldn't tell you about it even if I knew the details.*"

She walked to me and put her arms around me.

"*All those poor people.*

I only hope it brings the war to an end."

"*So do I. So do I.*"

We stood silently and just embraced one another.

CHAPTER THIRTY-TWO

Three days after the Japanese city of Hiroshima was destroyed by the first ever atomic bomb explosion, the United States was forced to detonate a second bomb, this time on the city of Nagasaki. Despite the devastation wrought by the first bomb and the revelation that such a weapon actually existed, the Japanese hierarchy refused to concede the war.

This time their response was different.

Realizing that they couldn't compete against such a force, and knowing that their manpower and supplies were dwindling, Emperor Hirohito and Prime Minister Suzuki immediately sought an end to hostilities.

On August 14, 1945, they accepted an unconditional surrender and General Douglas MacArthur was appointed head of the occupation forces in Japan.

On September 2, 1945, the Japanese formally signed the instrument of surrender aboard the USS Missouri in Tokyo Bay while a thousand carrier based aircraft flew overhead. Victory in Japan . . . VJ Day . . . was then formally declared by President Truman.

∽

"Well, it's over . . . finally" I said to Helen as the news was broadcast over the radio.

"Does this mean our days of train travel are at an end?"

"I think so . . . I hope so, and maybe we can start thinking about what we would like to do with our lives after I get out of the corps."

Helen looked at me in astonishment.

"I thought you were one of those 'once a Marine, always a Marine' type. Do you mean you'd actually consider getting out of the service?"

"That's an attitude, not necessarily a way of life" I said referring to the Marine remark.

"What would you like to do? We've never really talked about it.

War is all we've known practically since we met."

"It would be nice to go back near home, but then you're from the south. Maybe we can find somewhere sort of in between.

But what would you do?"

"Congress passed a bill last year that helps veterans return to school. I was thinking maybe I could go to college."

"But what would you like to study . . . I mean, do you know what you want to do with your life?

"I'll have to give that a lot of thought. But, we've got time. My enlistment isn't up until early next year, so it'll give us time to decide where we want to live and what I should consider for a career."

"Oh, Jim. I'm so proud of you."

She leaned in for a kiss.

I looked down at her expanding waist line.

"It's becoming hard to get close to you."

She just smiled a smile of contentment.

I arrived at headquarters early the next morning . . . after a night of revelry around Washington and across the nation. For the first time in over four years, people in the U.S. and around the world could actually begin thinking of a life without a world war overshadowing their every thought and action.

I was back by midday.

"They've got one more Victory tour planned, starting next week. It'll be the same basic circle that we made . . . out along the northern states, south

through California and back along the southern route ending up back here in D.C. Of course, we have to swing up through New England before we start west."

"Of course" Helen replied.

"But . . ." I lingered purposefully.

"But, there's a planned stop in Hartford for a full day. So, I was thinking perhaps we could arrange to see your family. It's been a long time. And if you don't want to make the full trip in your current delicate condition, you can stay with them for a while . . . or go back to D.C and wait for me."

"You're the most considerate man in the world. How did I ever get so lucky as to find you?"

"Actually, I'm the lucky one.

I found you, remember?"

She thought about that for a moment.

"Well, I'd have to say that we're just plain lucky we found each other.

About Hartford, I think I'd like to just arrange a brief visit with my family and then continue on the trip with you. You were gone a long time and I want to savor every moment we have together. After all, when you get out of the service and go back to school, you'll be busy with your studies . . . and I'll be busy with (looking down at her expanding waistline) this little person."

"That's great. It's what I had hoped you would say."

I motioned her toward me and put my arm around her.

I looked into her eyes.

"You are my soul mate. Don't ever leave my side."

Her expression changed to one of bewilderment.

"Why would I ever do that?"

I held her tighter.

"You're all I thought of all those lonely days and nights during my time in the Pacific. I was so afraid I'd never see you again. Now that we're together, I want it to stay that way always."

"It will, Jim.

It will."

✍

The final circle tour of the U.S. War Bond Drive commenced just before Thanksgiving, took just under four weeks and was touted a complete success. We arrived back home just before the Christmas holidays.

While the war was now officially over, America was in a celebratory mood and still generous to a fault in their contributions to the war cost reduction effort. Seeing her family briefly in Connecticut at the beginning of the tour had been nice, but Helen had come to the realization that her family was her past and I was her present and future.

She was just glad to be home. The pregnancy was progressing as was her abdominal girth and just getting up in the morning was becoming a chore. As we stepped from the train at Union Station, I held her hand. We were surprised to see some old friends awaiting our arrival.

Betty was there with her fiancé.

"Jim, Helen . . . this is Aaron."

I shook his hand but Helen couldn't resist an old fashioned hug.

"It's so nice to finally meet you. Betty has told us so much about you."

Helen stood back and admired the handsome man that Betty had managed to catch. Aaron was over six feet tall, slender with a slightly athletic build, wavy black hair and an almost baritone voice. And his blue eyes immediately caught everyone's attention.

"So you work for the Navy Department I understand?"

"Yes. I'm in their legal department. I presume Betty told you that I was in law school when the war broke out. Although I had just one year to go, I volunteered for service."

I immediately responded.

"That's quite patriotic of you. I'm always glad to hear of people who put country ahead of self."

"Well, it's nowhere near what you accomplished in the Pacific, but I'm glad to have done my part. I'm hoping to finish at Georgetown by next Christmas if I can get an early release and be accepted back for the spring semester."

"So you'll be right here in D.C. then?"

"That's where I did my first two years."

The women were chatting non-stop in the background when I turned toward them.

"Honey, don't you think we should head home?

It's been a long and thoroughly exhausting trip for you. Why don't we invite these two over for dinner one day next week? Then we can really catch up on things."

The ladies hugged and agreed that it would be best if Helen got some rest.

"I'll call you and we'll arrange to get together" Helen yelled as we got into the waiting cab.

Betty stood holding Aaron's hand and waving as the cab disappeared into the D.C. traffic.

✍

Next week never happened.

Helen had discussed inviting Betty and Aaron for dinner, but the following Saturday night a more pressing matter occurred.

Helen had just gone into the bathroom, when I heard her cry out. I rushed to the bathroom, only to find Helen straddling the toilet and a flood of water on the floor.

"My water just broke and I'm starting to have contractions."

I was startled at first, but then cooler heads prevailed.

"Should I call the hospital or did they advise you what to do?"

"They said if my water broke that I should go to the hospital to be checked. If it was just labor pains they had suggested waiting until they were about four minutes apart before coming since this is my first.

So . . . I guess we had better just get over there."

I immediately called Checker Cab and they said they would dispatch a vehicle right away. Helen already had a small suitcase ready . . . she had left it packed when we got home from the train trip earlier in the week . . . just in case.

Before ten minutes had elapsed, the cab driver was at the door.

"Take us to Providence Hospital" I commanded him.

"My wife is about to have our first child."

The driver put the car in gear and headed for the hospital without further ado.

"I remember our first" he said, while looking in the rearview mirror.

"Seems like only yesterday and now she's going to be twenty-five next month. We've got six all together."

I looked at Helen and smiled.

Helen caught my meaning but was in too much distress from the labor pains to return the smile.

"The pains are coming pretty often" she stated

"I don't think we're going to be any too early getting there."

✍

"Well, here we are" said the driver.

He jumped out of the cab and ran into the hospital entrance and momentarily was back with a wheelchair. I helped Helen into the chair and wheeled her quickly to the admitting desk.

"This is my wife, Helen Mathews" I said to the clerk.

"Her obstetrician is Dr. Robert Lowry."

The clerk made a quick call.

"Someone will be here in just a moment to take you to maternity. They will check you there and then call your doctor."

Practically before we could turn around, an attendant in white pants and shirt appeared.

"Mrs. Mathews, I'm Carl" the black man said.

"So you're ready to have your baby?" he said with a big grin that showed a mouth full of pearly white teeth.

"Follow us", he said turning to me.

After an elevator trip to the fourth floor, he took Helen through a door where the nurses were expecting her.

"There's a waiting room with chairs just down the hall to your left" he said to me while pointing the direction.

"The nurses will be out shortly to let you know how she's doing."

I walked to the waiting area and took a seat. The room was empty.

As I sat there, I thought about what a year it had been. The battles that I had been in and the death and destruction that I had witnessed. I recalled the feelings I had when I had been rescued on Iwo Jima and when I found out that I was to be awarded the Medal of Honor. And the ceremony itself at the White House when I was presented the medal by President Truman, with the Commandant of the Marine Corps looking on.

But somehow those experiences didn't compare to the feelings I had right that minute when I was about to become a father for the first time.

"Mr. Mathews?"

"I'm Captain Mathews" I said to the nurse addressing me.

"Your wife is doing fine. She is already about six centimeters dilated, so it shouldn't be too long. She's moving along very quickly for a first pregnancy."

I'm sure I looked a little puzzled.

"Ten centimeters is fully dilated" the nurse retorted. She could undoubtedly see the perplexed look on my face when she told me 'six centimeters'."

"Dr. Lowry is already on his way. I'm sure he will be out to see you just as soon as he arrives and has a chance to examine your wife."

"May I see my wife now?"

"We're getting her ready for the doctor. He's usually here within ten or fifteen minutes, so you shouldn't have to wait long. He usually allows husbands to stay with their wives during labor."

"Thank you."

I took my seat and picked up a magazine although I couldn't concentrate on the article I had opened to. Fortunately, I didn't have to wait long. As the nurse had suggested, Dr. Lowry was there within minutes and soon presented himself in the waiting area.

"Captain, your wife is progressing nicely. If she keeps this up, I expect you'll have your new son or daughter within the next hour or two. In the meantime, why don't you come on back to her room? I'm sure she could use a little moral support.

We've given her a mild sedative to help the pains, but she may not be in quite the mood you are used to."

I caught his meaning. I had been forewarned about women during labor . . . they often say and do things that they don't really mean and usually don't remember having said or done after the baby has arrived.

"You're the cause of all this" she yelled at me as I entered the labor room.

I thought to myself that she was there as was I when the baby was conceived but I thought better and decided to hold back any retorts I might be formulating. Instead, I took her hand and leaned over and kissed her forehead.

"The doctor says you're doing nicely and we should have our baby soon."

"That's easy for him to say. He's not the one having these terrible pains."

She grimaced as she began another contraction.

The nurse stood on the other side of the bed from me and continued to encourage Helen.

"Jim, if you wouldn't mind stepping out for a moment, I'd like to check your wife again." Dr. Lowry said upon reentering the room.

"Sure" I said as I aimed for the door. Just then Helen let out a scream.

"Quick" said Dr. Lowry, "let's get her to the delivery room. She's crowning."

Again I looked bewildered.

Dr. Lowry interpreted the look on my face and added:

"The baby's head is beginning to show. You'll be a father very shortly."

An orderly arrived from out of nowhere and helped move the bed down the hall to the delivery room where Helen was quickly transferred to the delivery table.

Dr. Lowry suddenly reappeared with gown and gloves.

"You're doing just splendidly. Now, take a deep breath, hold it and then let's have a big push."

Although she was obviously in pain, Helen complied.

"One or two like that and it'll all be over."

Helen was perspiring profusely, but she repeated her effort and suddenly a baby's cry broke the silence.

"It's a girl" Dr. Lowry proudly announced as he held the baby up by its feet and handed her to the nurse. She placed our daughter into a blanket and held her in front of Helen.

"Can I hold her?"

The nurse smiled.

"Of course, she's all yours."

Helen took her into her arms.

I stood next to Helen admiring our new daughter.

"She's beautiful" we uttered in unison.

"Have you decided on a name yet?" Dr. Lowry queried.

"Maria."

"That's a beautiful name. It suits her well and it goes nicely with Mathews. Is there a middle name?"

"Yes. Lynn.

Maria Lynn Mathews."

Helen and I held hands as we peered down at our new creation.

Meanwhile, Dr. Lowry repaired the episiotomy that had been a necessary adjunct to the delivery. Helen didn't blink as he injected some medication to numb the area.

"Well, I'm all done here" he said as he took off his gloves.

"Let's get you back to your room. I suspect you've had quite a day and probably deserve a little rest. When you're ready, the nurse will take young Maria to the nursery. One of our baby doctors would like to check her and make sure everything is all right, although she appears perfect."

CHAPTER THIRTY-THREE

Maria was perfect and was home with her proud parents within five days of her birth.

There was a brief interlude on the screen and then suddenly Jim was back.

"Well, that's my story . . . our story . . . and you my darling Helen (and Maria if you are there) know the rest of it and sadly how it has now ended for me.

But know that if there is a heaven . . . and if that's where I am now, that I'm thinking of you and will be waiting for you when your time comes."

As he turned to walk away from the camera, sounds of the Marine Corps Hymn gradually became louder in the background:

"From the halls of Montezuma
To the shores of Tripoli
We will fight our countries battles
On the land and on the sea."

❦

Maria turned to her mother and gently put her head on her shoulder.
Both women were in tears.

"That's the most moving tribute your father could have left us. He was a great man and I think we should approach someone about making this into a book about his life."

Maria assured her mother that she would consult some of her acquaintances in the publishing business.

"I think almost anyone with a love of history especially as it involves America's wars and her heroes will want to read Dad's story."

"I hope so" replied Helen.

"I do hope so!"

EPILOGUE

The following was added by Maria with Helen's help. Now almost seventy five and with some health issues, she was glad to have a daughter with a background in literature.

Dad made no specific reference to his eventual life's work. After he retired from the Corps, he used the GI bill to return to college at Duke University where he earned a degree in education. He and Helen decided on settling in the small town of Lawrenceville, Georgia where Jim helped improve the secondary school system that was just transitioning from three to four year high school making it competitive with other states. He taught U.S. and world history and was eventually to serve as principal of Lawrenceville High School and later the first school superintendant of Gwinnett County combined schools.

He was approached by some of his colleagues and asked if he would consider running for state superintendant of education, but declined as he was never comfortable outside the local arena. Similarly, he participated in *local/regional military affairs, especially on Memorial Day annually as a medal winner, but declined offers to speak at national assemblies.*

When asked about his time in the war, his answer always remained the same: "I wish my fellow soldiers could share this honor with me (referring to the medal). They deserve the accolades that I have been given far more than me since they gave their last measure of devotion on those Pacific islands."

Then he would always conclude with "Semper Fi".

It was always heartwarming to see the Marines in attendance stand and render a salute while tears were streaming from their eyes.

He was a quiet man, but a great man who will be missed by all who knew him.

It was for these reasons that Mom and I decided to put his story down on paper for publication. With the help of several Marine organizations his story became widely publicized and was welcomed when it finally was published by a major literary company.

Jim's story, entitled "Heroes of the Pacific", about the men of the 4th Marine Division and their campaigns at Saipan, Tinian, Iwo Jima and Roi-Namur went on to sell well over 100,000 copies in book, VCR and eventually CD-Rom format.

-End